MURDER ON EATON SQUARE

SQUARE

A GINGER GOLD MYSTERY # 10

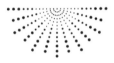

LEE STRAUSS

Library and Archives Canada Cataloguing in Publication Title: Murder on Eaton Square: a cozy historical 1920s mystery / Lee Strauss. Names: Strauss, Lee (Novelist), author. Series: Strauss, Lee (Novelist). Ginger Gold mystery ; 10. Description: Series statement: A Ginger Gold mystery ; 10 Identifiers: Canadiana (print) 20190131799 | Canadiana (ebook) 20190131802 | ISBN 9781774090374 (softcover) | ISBN 9781774090381 (hardcover) | ISBN 9781774090398 (IngramSpark softcover) | ISBN 9781774090299 (Kindle) | ISBN 9781774090367 (Epub) Classification: LCC PS8637.T739 M88 2019 | DDC C813/.6—dc23

GINGER GOLD MYSTERIES

(IN ORDER)

*M*rs. Ginger Reed, alias Lady Gold, had reserved a box at the London Playhouse Theatre for her family, who now, mingling with anticipation and glasses of champagne in hand, waited for the signal that the production of Shakespeare's *Romeo & Juliet* was about to begin.

"I never grow tired of living in London!" Felicia Gold said. Felicia, Ginger's exuberant and *très* modern former sister-in-law, was the sister of Ginger's late husband, Daniel, Lord Gold, and what Ginger's American counterparts would now, in the year 1925, call a super-flapper. Indeed, Felicia looked the epitome of the icon in a beaded, sleeveless frock with a lantern fringe that barely landed mid-shin. Her glossy auburn bob was pressed down with a glittering headband to which a large feather was attached. "My darling, Ginger," Felicia went on. "Thank you from the bottom of my heart for rescuing me from dull country living!"

"I quite miss the quiet of the country," said Ginger's former grandmother, the Dowager Lady Gold. "Young people at least had manners and knew their place in proper society." She scowled at Felicia's outfit and the bare skin shown, but refrained from speaking out her displeasure at Felicia's flagrant display in the presence of strangers who could possibly overhear. Ambrosia had tried to enter the twentieth century by having her long hair cut into a short shingle, but her spirit hadn't quite made it over. "My heart is rather broken over the loss of Bray Manor."

"Oh bosh, Grandmama," Felicia said, brightly. "I fear that your loss is my gain."

Ginger pulled on her husband's arm, subtly separating the two Gold ladies. Chief Inspector Basil Reed's mouth twitched, and his handsome hazel eyes glinted in amusement. Ginger was glad to see Basil found the situation humorous.

"I don't think I've had a chance to say it before now," he said, "but you are a sight of loveliness."

Ginger felt the weight of the tiara she wore on her head—red hair in a stylish marcelled bob—which went perfectly with her sequin-covered gown.

"Thank you, love," Ginger said, but before she

could return the compliment, their attention was captured by the group occupying the box next to them.

"I wish I'd stayed at home." The voice belonged to a gruff-sounding gentleman in a wheelchair. "I can't stand theatre."

"Why did you come then?" An attractive woman in her forties shot the man a disparaging look.

"Because you'd never let me hear the end of it if I didn't. You and your endless social engagements! You're going to put me in the grave before God is through with me."

Basil whispered into Ginger's ear. "That's Mr. Reginald Peck and his second wife, Mrs. Virginia Peck."

"Of Eaton Square?" Ginger said. "We're attending a gala at their house tomorrow evening."

"Which would explain Mr. Peck's complaint."

"And the others with them?"

"They are his children by his first wife. The young man dressed in that fine suit is his son, Matthew, and the young lady is his daughter, Mrs. Deirdre Northcott."

The two siblings were dressed as one might do for a night at the theatre, similarly to their father and step-mother, in a fine suit and a gorgeous evening gown.

"Who's the other fellow?" A third man was dressed as if he were a visiting dignitary from India, in a brown satin pyjama-style *kurta*. However, the pale tones of his skin and hair belied Indian ethnicity.

"That is the son-in-law, Alistair Northcott."

"How eclectic," Ginger said. "I suppose we shouldn't be rude and not greet them. I would like the hosts to recognise me when we show up at their gala."

Basil led Ginger by her elbow to the end of their box that joined with the Peck family's. Virginia Peck spotted them and made strides to greet them. Ginger, an expert in all the top fashion designers, recognised the Elsa Schiaparelli gown immediately.

"Good evening," Mrs. Peck said. "It's Mr. Basil Reed, is it not?"

"Indeed," Basil said.

Before Basil could introduce Ginger, Mrs. Peck continued, "I've met your parents, Mr. Reed. They share mutual friends with my husband, Reginald." Her eyes darted to the man in the wheelchair, positioned at the opposite end to where Mrs. Peck had sat. Mr. Matthew Peck and Mr. and Mrs. Northcott sat in the chairs between them.

"I hear they're back in the city," Mrs. Peck said. "Such adventurers!"

"Indeed, they are," Basil said.

"I quite envy them."

"Yes," Basil shifted and changed the subject. "May I introduce my wife, Ginger Reed?"

Mrs. Peck finally looked Ginger in the eye and offered a tired smile. "Forgive me. I do get carried away at times. How do you do?"

"Very well, thank you," Ginger said. "We received an invitation to your gala and I saw I had a unique opportunity to make your acquaintance beforehand."

"I host the gala every year to raise funds for our injured servicemen. Our own Matthew was injured in the fighting. She cast a glance at her stepson and lowered her voice. "He's never been quite the same since returning, I'm afraid. But let's not be solemn on such a fabulous evening. I'm delighted you can make it tomorrow, and I look forward to seeing you again."

The lights dimmed signalling the production was about to begin.

"Enjoy the show, Mrs. Peck," Basil said.

"Likewise."

Once they were seated, Ginger spoke softly, "She seems lovely, though I get the feeling she's not very happy."

"I don't think Reginald Peck is the easiest fellow to live with. He's had ongoing health problems. I'm dreadfully sorry to see he's ended up in a wheelchair."

"A house on Eaton Square—he must be a very wealthy man."

"Oh yes. He built his wealth buying and selling

5

property and is apparently quite savvy with the stock market."

The curtains parted, and Ginger, along with a myriad of other spectators, lifted a small set of viewing glasses to her eyes. It just so happened that the angle allowed her a quick study of the intriguing family in the box next door. Everyone's eyes were on the stage except for Mr. Matthew Peck's. He was most definitely glaring at his brother-in-law—or was he staring at his father? Mr. Reginald Peck and Mr. Northcott were seated side by side. At any rate, if *looks could kill*. Ginger shivered and focused on the action on stage, quite determined to mind her own business.

CHAPTER TWO

*T*aking a few minutes to gather her pink summer Kashalyne coat, which was trimmed smartly with red silk ribbon, and her simple, red satin cloche hat, Ginger called for her Boston terrier, Boss, and headed to the garage in the back garden of Hartigan House where her '24 Crossley was parked. It was a fairly new acquisition, and Ginger felt proud to be the owner. The glossy white exterior and complementary dark red leather interior, along with the polished mahogany dashboard, had a sophistication about it. She reversed out of the garage and puttered down the narrow lane.

Arriving at her office on Watson Street, Ginger parked with one tyre tight to the kerb, climbed out of the Crossley, and hurried along the pavement. Boss trotted at her heels. Seeing the new sign above the door

—Lady Gold Investigations—gave Ginger a silent thrill. And with it only being just around the corner from her dress shop, Feathers & Flair, the convenience couldn't be denied.

It was always a toss-up as to which business she should check in with first. When a new shipment of fabrics or frocks was due, the fashion shop was the obvious choice, but the investigations office held the promise of intrigue. Had someone come in with a tantalising problem? Was Felicia sitting on the edge of her seat waiting for Ginger to arrive so she could tell her about the mysterious potential client?

Since no delivery was scheduled for the dress shop, and her parking spot was next to the investigation office, her decision was simple. She descended the steps into the shallow well that led to the office entrance and proceeded through the small waiting room.

A light-toned bell rang as she turned the brass knob and pushed the wooden door open. Felicia jumped to her feet, and Ginger prepared herself for a new case.

Once the previous tenant had vacated, Ginger's hired decorators had done an excellent job creating a perfect office space suitable for an investigator. Uncluttered, yet classy, the walls were papered in a bright beige and gold design resembling interlocking fans, a red rug warmed the wooden floor, and the windows, now cleaned, allowed a good amount of natural light in. Ginger's walnut desk sat prominently to one side with wine-coloured leather chairs for clients facing it and a wicker dog bed for Boss tucked out of sight behind it. Felicia's desk sat at a right angle to Ginger's so they could easily converse. A small kitchen, the lavatory, and a darkroom were hidden away down a corridor.

Felicia snapped to attention at Ginger's arrival. "Oh, thank goodness you're here!"

"What is it? Has someone come in with a plea?"

"No. That's the problem. I'm bored silly."

Disappointed, Ginger sighed softly. "I thought you were working on your book." Felicia had recently sold a mystery novel to a London publisher and was now wrestling through the second volume.

"I am. At least I'm trying." Felicia let out a soulful moan. "I just can't see past this white page! I'm so close to the ending, but something in my mind is blocked."

"Perhaps you need a change of scenery and a bit of fresh air," Ginger said. "Why don't you see if the girls need help at the shop?"

Felicia stuck out her lower lip in protest, but before she could say anything, the telephone rang. She answered with a look of hope in her eyes.

"Lady Gold Investigations." Felicia's eyes darted to

Ginger. "Yes? I'm afraid Lady Gold isn't available. Might I take a message?"

The man's voice was loud enough for Ginger to hear but not enough to understand what he was saying.

"I'm sure she can help you with that, sir. I'll jot down your name and telephone number if you recite it now."

Ginger watched as Felicia scribbled the information on a blank pad.

Felicia's grey eyes flashed as she lowered the receiver and ended the call. "It's a case. A simple surveillance. The sister claims to have got a job, and the brother, a Mr. Soames, wants to make sure she's going to work like she says. I think he suspects her of a romantic assignation."

"Oh dear."

"Please, Ginger, let me do it," the enthusiasm in Felicia's voice was palpable. "I can ask around and then bring you the information. I'll be discreet, I promise. Besides, I need real-life experiences to stir up fresh inspiration for my book."

"Do you think you can rein in your excitement?" Ginger said with a note of seriousness. "The key to successful sleuthing is to not draw attention to one's self."

Felicia's shoulders went limp, and her facial expression bland.

"I don't mean to disappoint—"

"Ah-ah!" Felicia said. "You were immediately fooled. I can control my exuberance when the situation calls for it. Let me prove it to you."

"Very well," Ginger said. It wasn't as if Felicia could mess it up too terribly. At worst, they'd lose a client Ginger didn't truly want anyway.

Felicia hopped on the toes of her T-strap shoes, then immediately subdued herself. "Don't forget that I'm an actress, Ginger. I shall become a detective to challenge Sherlock Holmes. A chameleon, I tell you."

Ginger waved her fingers. "Off you go, then."

"Oh, can I borrow the Crossley?"

Ginger snorted at her sister-in-law's audacity. "I think you can solve this case quite well taking a bus or the underground."

Felicia was too delighted about her first lead investigation to be put off by Ginger's pronouncement for long. She grabbed her handbag and paused at the mirror by the door to don her hat. It was a new blue cloche with a simple but stylish broad black leather band. "A taxicab it is!" she announced, before disappearing.

CHAPTER THREE

*G*inger had little reason for envy, but a house in Eaton Square would be frightfully divine. The white stone Victorian buildings were statuesque in appearance, slender and tall, and five storeys in total. Three floors of glamorous living sat above the cellar level where the servants worked, and were topped with an attic, which housed the sleeping quarters for the same.

Pristine gardens ran the length of the townhouses and mirrored the Buckingham Palace Gardens only a short walk away.

"Winston Churchill lives here," Basil said when they arrived later that evening at the gala hosted by the esteemed Peck family. "And Mr. Baldwin's home is on Eaton Square as well, when he's not living in Downing Street."

Ginger was duly impressed that the Pecks had both the chancellor of the exchequer and the prime minister as neighbours.

The interior of the Pecks' house captured Ginger's imagination. It seemed money was no object as every single piece of furniture and art were of the best quality from the very top artists and designers. It was all rather tropical, as there appeared to be more flower arrangements than guests, who were numerous.

"It must've cost a fortune to import all these flower arrangements." Ginger held on to Basil's arm.

"You'd be surprised to hear that Mr. Reginald Peck has rather green fingers," Basil returned. "In fact, he had a conservatory built on the rooftop, quite extraordinary, since no one on Eaton Square had ever done such a thing. Rather scandalous when it was being built and the news made several of the rags, though that was quite a few years ago now. Quite forgotten by most."

Wearing a ball gown of gold lace over a gold lamé slip dress, Ginger caught the eye of more than one envious woman or appreciative man. It had a daringly low, square-cut neckline, and a long decorative hem that landed just below the knee. A matching scarf wrapped around her neck and hung long over her right shoulder. The metallic fibres glistened under the electric lamps, and Ginger couldn't help feeling illuminated. One simply could not overdress for such an event as this. Basil, of course, looked ravishing in his black evening suit and top hat with a contrasting white silk waistcoat and bow tie.

"If only Hartigan House had been built in Belgravia," Ginger said after a sip of champagne.

Basil patted her gloved hand and consoled her. "South Kensington is a splendid place to live, as well."

"But just imagine running into His Majesty whilst riding past Buckingham Palace. Or Queen Mary. I hear she loves to ride."

"All royals ride, my dear," Basil said. "Equestrian arts are highly esteemed among the elite." He smiled at her and added, "As you know."

Ginger knew Basil was referring to her spectacular gelding, Goldmine, and his own exceptional Arabian, Sir Blackwell.

"We are not elite," Ginger said. "At least, I'm not." Anymore. Ginger had given up her role as a baroness and her official title of "Lady Gold" when she married Basil Reed. Before her marriage to Daniel Gold, Ginger had been a commoner, albeit from fortunate circumstances. Basil could boast of being the son of an "Honourable". Which reminded Ginger.

"Basil, have your parents confirmed that they're coming for dinner tomorrow?"

"Oh, yes, I received a letter from them this morning. Sorry I didn't mention it. It slipped my mind. They're looking forward to meeting you."

Ginger was interested in them as well but worried that they might not take to her. From what Basil had mentioned, the Honourable Henry Reed, also known as Harry, and Mrs. Anna Reed were rather old fashioned and felt gentry wives had no business being in a place of employment.

An energetic five-piece orchestral band from America occupied the ballroom's centre stage. Lush palms were placed on either side, adding to the gala's tropical ambience.

The music was a mix of standard waltzes and more lively, modern dance numbers.

Ginger loved to dance with Basil, who was a natural talent on the dance floor. One of her earliest memories of her husband was when they'd shared a dance on the SS *Rosa* before they had even been formally introduced. They were masters of the foxtrot, and Ginger couldn't help but notice others admiring them now as they danced.

An older couple swayed past, and the lady was heard to proclaim, "We were once young and beautiful, Arthur."

The gentleman responded, "Where has the time gone?"

Ginger smiled up at Basil.

"That is Lord and Lady Clifford," he said. "They live next door."

Ginger and Basil finished the dance laughing and feeling euphoric.

"Such fun!" Ginger said. A parlour maid walked by with a tray of drinks, and Ginger and Basil helped themselves to fresh glasses of champagne. Ginger caught the eye of their hostess, Mrs. Peck, who was watching them. Looking rather forlorn, Mrs. Peck stood by her husband.

Ginger nudged Basil. "Why don't you ask Mrs. Peck to dance?" Virginia Peck was impeccably dressed in a gorgeous Parisian gown. She had a way of looking both refined and worldly, though a hint of melancholy shadowed her.

"She looks so unsettled," Ginger said, "for someone who must've spent weeks planning this event."

Basil inclined his head. "If you don't mind?"

"Of course not. I'll see to cheering up Mr. Peck."

The dour expression on the older man's well-lined face spoke of his lack of enthusiasm for the party, something he'd complained loudly about the night before, so Ginger thought it must've been an act of love for his wife, that he'd agreed to attend.

Before Ginger made it to Mr. Peck's side, the host was approached by a man in possession of a long face and serious expression. Ginger slowed her steps but couldn't help overhearing.

"I tell you it's true!" Mr. Peck said. "If I wanted a solicitor to do my thinking for me, I'd have hired someone else."

The man's lips tightened at the rebuke. He bowed slightly and walked away.

Ginger continued her approach and pretended she hadn't witnessed the uncomfortable exchange. "Good evening, Mr. Peck." She settled into an empty chair next to him and sipped her champagne. "We haven't had a chance to be officially introduced. I'm Mrs. Reed, the wife of Chief Inspector Reed."

He nodded without a hint of a smile. "I thought you must be the new Mrs. Reed. I see your husband has attached himself to my wife."

"Basil loves to dance," Ginger said playfully. "Wasn't the performance last night marvellous? Did you enjoy it?"

Mr. Peck grunted. "I already know enough about family squabbles; I don't have to pay good money to see it played out for me on the stage."

Ginger was a little surprised that Mr. Peck would be so forthright about his feelings about his own family.

"Still, it's a nice escape to witness problems that aren't your own," she said.

"It always ends in tragedy, Mrs. Reed. Mark my words."

Oh mercy.

Not to be deterred by open negativity, Ginger pressed on. "Such a wonderful party and a fabulous cause. It's my understanding Mrs. Peck hosts this fundraiser every year?"

"Unfortunately, yes."

"You don't support the cause?"

"Of course I support the cause. I see the 'cause' in front of me every day."

Ginger could only assume Mr. Peck was referring to his son, Matthew.

"I think it's someone else's turn to pick up the torch and sponsor the event," he added. "A man can't get a day's rest around here."

"Yes, well, it's my first time attending," Ginger said, intending to keep the conversation light. "I'm quite new to London."

"I know," he said without warmth. "I read about your return in the papers."

Mr. Peck had his eyes locked on his wife, and Ginger hoped that Basil's invitation to dance hadn't upset the man.

"They're both quite good," Ginger said. "Aren't they?"

"I don't trust the Met."

"Oh. Well, Basil works for the CID at Scotland Yard." Ginger knew she was splitting hairs, but she couldn't help but feel a little defensive.

Mr. Peck settled his gaze on Ginger. "I knew your father."

Ginger worked to hold in her surprise, not only at the sudden change of subject but at the statement itself. Though it made sense. Her late father, George Hartigan, and Mr. Peck would have been around the same age, mid- to late-sixties, and her father had a reputation for having been a brilliant businessman during the years he'd resided in London.

When Reginald Peck didn't elaborate, Ginger felt at a loss. "I knew him too" would have been an inappropriate response. Asking him how he'd known her father might open up an opportunity for Mr. Peck to say something less than flattering, and Ginger didn't want to risk that. Not that her father had a poor reputation, only that her host didn't seem bent on seeing the good in people.

The dance ended, and Ginger was glad to have an excuse to leave Mr. Peck's side.

"I think I'll mingle, Mr. Peck. I'm sure we'll meet again sometime."

"If I live that long. Good evening, Mrs. Reed."

Ginger was quite astounded at Mr. Peck's flippant

reference to his poor health and wondered just how ill the man was.

She reached Basil's side just as Mrs. Peck was taking her leave. "Thank you, Chief Inspector Reed. It was delightful."

Shortly after, Ginger and Basil were taking a turn about the room when a bout of arguing from the foyer reached their ears.

Her interest piqued, Ginger arched a brow and said, "Shall we investigate?"

They entered the foyer in time to see Matthew Peck poke Alastair Northcott in the chest with his finger.

"You should've stayed in India, Northcott!"

"So you could fill your father's head with lies?"

"Lies? You're the one posing as a ridiculous Indian guru, *Arjun.*"

"At least I'm not obsessed with getting my hands on your father's money."

"What goes on between me and my father is none of your damned business!"

"He's Deirdre's father too."

"Enough!" Mr. Peck's voice boomed loudly and clearly. How he'd got there so quickly was evident by the butler pushing his wheelchair. Though seated, it was apparent by the length of Mr. Peck's torso and limbs that he was a tall man. He would have quite likely once borne down upon the heads of his children in his anger. Even from his lower position, his authority remained undiminished, and the men responded by breaking away.

Deirdre Northcott, looking rather pale, took Mr. Northcott by the arm. "Alastair. You've made a scene."

Mr. Peck peered at the small crowd circling the two men with a look of regret, then made demands of his butler. "Take me to my room."

The butler did as commanded and pushed his master down the corridor beyond the staircase, to where Ginger assumed a lift must be located.

Ginger mumbled into Basil's ear. "Every family has its secrets."

CHAPTER FOUR

*T*he breakfast table in the morning room at Hartigan House was a beehive of activity. Mrs. Beasley, their stout cook with her perpetually pink face, was a master in the kitchen. Lizzie, the parlour maid and sometimes lady's maid for Ginger, produced a plate of sizzling bacon followed by a dish of scrambled eggs. Already waiting on the sideboard were sausages, a plate of grilled tomatoes, and pots of tea and dark coffee.

"It looks and smells delicious," Basil said. "Please let Mrs. Beasley know."

Ginger smiled at her new husband. He appreciated good food served regularly and appeared to be adjusting well to a full house, and one where three headstrong Gold women abided.

Ambrosia's presence was preceded by the tapping

of her silver-headed walking stick along the wooden floor. Ginger suspected that the matriarch disliked that she must always announce her own arrival.

"Good morning," Ambrosia said politely. She nodded subtly to Ginger and Basil and ignored the small lad who sat to Ginger's side.

Scout Elliot's place at the table was a recent adjustment for all. A street waif, Ginger had brought the lad, now eleven, under her roof and had become his official guardian. Currently, she was in the legal process of making Scout her and Basil's adoptive son.

Ambrosia had a difficult time with the newest family member and refused to look the youngster in the eye. The feathers of the serving staff were also ruffled since the child they'd taken to bossing about would have authority to do the same to them. Scout would become "Master Scout".

Ginger understood the social struggle as an English lady, but as an American, she found the whole system quite tiresome, and she wasn't about to let an archaic class system keep her from experiencing the joys of motherhood. Fate had brought Scout into her life, and her heart had opened with a floodgate of love that could not be stopped or reversed.

Like an exotic bird newly freed from its cage, Felicia fluttered into the room. She wore a Japanese silk kimono, and floated onto an empty chair opposite her grandmother.

"I finished the edits my editor has been waiting for," she announced.

"I'm so happy for you," Ginger said with sincerity.

Felicia's new career as a mystery writer had brought on a positive change and had seemed to pull her from the tendency towards self-destructive behaviours. She was even turning out to be a reliable help at the new business office of Lady Gold Investigations. Felicia had mentioned enjoying her new position at Ginger's office because it provided peace and quiet for her writing, something hard to come by at Hartigan House.

"Shall I take Boss for a walk?" Scout asked.

Boss had an enviable position between Ginger and Scout and sat obediently on his haunches hoping for a bit of bacon and egg.

"Perfect," Ginger said.

"May I clean up after Goldmine whilst I'm out?"

The staff weren't the only ones who had difficulty with Scout's new status. Scout himself preferred the hard bunk in the attic to the soft bed down the hall from Ginger and Basil, sponge baths under the lenient hand of Lizzie to Ginger's insistence on full immersion in the bathtub at regular intervals, and fewer educational lessons than were now on his agenda.

Ginger smiled patiently and said, "Of course."

She sighed as she watched him go.

Basil put a comforting hand on her arm. "You knew it would be difficult. Big changes take time to adjust to."

"I know," Ginger said. Adopting Scout was something she wanted more than anything else at the moment, but deep inside, she wondered if she was doing the right thing. Oh mercy! Of course, she was. Scout had a future now. This was the right thing.

Having finished her tea and toast, Ambrosia excused herself. "I've agreed to play bridge with Mrs. Schofield's club this morning." Mrs. Schofield was an elderly widow who lived in the residence next door. "That woman is like a dog with a bone; she insists I indulge in such frivolity."

Ginger smiled as she watched the Dowager Lady Gold leave. She walked as tall as she could with the help of her walking stick. She and Mrs. Schofield had a strange but long-lasting friendship, and Ginger had no doubt that Ambrosia looked forward to the bridge club. Mrs. Schofield had let it slip that Ambrosia was a competitive player.

Pippins, Ginger's beloved, longtime butler, entered with the morning newspapers folded atop a silver platter. In his seventies, Pippins had bright cornflower eyes and was still in possession of the vim and vigour of a man a decade younger. Only his balding head and the slight bowing of his shoulders reflected his actual years.

"I'd like *The Times* please, Pips," Ginger said.

Basil, grinning slightly, picked up *The Daily News*.

Felicia commented wryly, "You lovebirds make fighting over a rag look romantic."

Ginger cast a glance Felicia's way before, quite unintentionally, she and Basil opened their selection to the front pages in tandem. Ginger gasped and shared a knowing look with Basil. Each paper ran the same story.

MR. REGINALD PECK OF EATON SQUARE FOUND DEAD.

CHAPTER FIVE

*B*asil pushed away from the table. "I need to get to the Yard."

It surprised Ginger a call hadn't come through already. The press could be like that, swooping in on news and printing it before the actual facts reached the police.

Basil kissed Ginger goodbye and hurried away. She called after him, "Do ring me later!"

"What is it?" Felicia said. "The world's not ending is it?"

Ginger turned the paper around so Felicia could read it.

"Mr. Reginald Peck died?"

"Apparently," Ginger said. She wouldn't have been surprised if the papers had got it wrong, or if it were some kind of hoax to drive sales.

"Weren't you just at a party at his house last night?"

"Yes," Ginger said. "It was quite an affair. You would've liked it."

"Drat! If not for this deadline looming, I would've been there."

"Sacrifices have to be made to follow your dreams, love."

"True."

"Poor Virginia Peck." Ginger added a teaspoon of sugar to her tea and stirred. "This must come as such a shock, though, I have to concede that the man didn't look well. He certainly seemed unhappy."

"You spoke to him?"

"Yes," Ginger said after a sip of tea. "The chap was frightfully sullen. Not to speak ill of the dead, of course."

Boss bounded in with Scout behind him. The lad was almost twelve years old but was small in size and looked closer to ten.

"All's done and cleaned up, missus."

Ginger moved from her place at the table, bent to scrub Boss behind the ears, and looked Scout in the eyes. "You're to call me Mum now, Scout."

Scout's gaze fell to the floor. One thing Ginger loved about her ward—her son (she too, had to grow accustomed to new titles)—was how cheerful he remained despite life's often hard offerings.

"I know it feels odd," Ginger said. "How about we start with Missus Mum?"

Ginger could sense Felicia's mirth and didn't miss the dark brow that inched up as she watched.

"Okay," Scout said. "Missus Mum. Shall I help Mr. Clement trim the lawns?"

Ginger shook her head. "The new tutor is coming today. A Mr. Fulton. He'll be here shortly. After your studies, you can play in the gardens."

"Play?" Scout looked sincerely perplexed. "Play wiv what, Missus Mum."

Ginger's heart felt bruised at the thought of her ward's lost childhood. "Ask Pippins. He knows games like I Spy and Noughts and Crosses. I'll speak to him for you. Just be nice to Mr. Fulton, and do as he says."

"Yes, Missus Mum."

Scout lumbered out like he didn't know who he was anymore, and Ginger sighed.

Felicia cupped a palm over Ginger's hand. "I know you are very fond of young Scout, but are you sure about this? He seems to be such a fish out of water."

Ginger sighed again. "I *have* to be sure, Felicia. I'm his only hope. What's his future going to look like if I give up?" What she didn't say was how would she ever be a mother, since providence hadn't smiled down on her that way.

"What about Marvin?" Felicia said.

Marvin Elliot was Scout's older cousin. Street children like Marvin and Scout had no skills and few job prospects. Many didn't even make it to adulthood.

"Who knows where Marvin would be now if I hadn't arranged for him to join the navy," Ginger said. Navy life wasn't easy, but it gave Marvin a chance to learn working skills and pursue a rather prestigious career. It took him off the streets and out of a life of crime.

Felicia picked up the paper Ginger had tossed aside and read the article. "When the butler entered to rouse Mr. Peck for breakfast, he found him dead in bed. A heart attack, they say."

"How unfortunate that the last thing you witness the night before you die is an awful row between your children," Ginger said.

"Wait." Felicia squinted. "You didn't mention a row, Ginger. That's the kind of thing that makes a stuffy event like that interesting. Now I really wish I'd gone!"

Ginger laughed. "You are quite easily entertained."

"I'm not. I'm only looking for ideas for my stories. You never know what will spark the next moment of inspiration."

"I can tell you the details later." Ginger checked her watch. "Mr. Fulton is to arrive any moment."

"What is this Mr. Fulton like?" Felicia asked. "For Scout's sake, I hope he's not an old grump."

"Not at all. Mr. William Fulton is in his thirties, a graduate of University College, London."

"Sounds like a bore."

"Not at all, if you thrive in academia." Ginger chose to ignore Felicia's snobbery. "I find intellect rather attractive."

"Oh, now you've got my curiosity aroused."

"Hardly, I'm sure."

"Very well." Felicia dropped her linen napkin on the food remnants on her plate. "I'll go and waste away my time at Lady Gold Investigations. Hopefully, an interesting client will come in. Preferably tall, dark, and handsome."

"And single, I assume," Ginger said, lightly.

"*That*," Felicia said with flair, "goes without saying. At any rate, I can work on my edits. That dratted deadline!"

Pippins stepped inside. "Mr. Fulton has arrived, madam. Should I ask him to wait in the sitting room?"

"Yes please, Pips. Also, before you go, I'm wondering if I might ask a favour?"

"Of course, madam. Anything."

"Do you remember how, when I was a child, we played simple games together?"

The corners of the butler's eyes crinkled as he smiled at the memory. "I do, madam."

"Would you mind terribly engaging young Scout in some play? It would mean so much to me."

To Ginger's relief, Pippins' expression remained accepting. "I'd be delighted."

INDEED, Mr. William Fulton had been one of many possible tutors Ginger had vetted in her quest, and the assessment she shared with Felicia was quite accurate. Serious, but not stern or gloomy, mature, but with a youthful spirit, Ginger hoped Mr. Fulton would be a long-standing person of value in Scout's life.

He stood as she entered the sitting room. He wore a trim beige suit, crisp white shirt with a stiff collar, and a classy bow tie, slightly askew. In one hand, he held a felt trilby hat. Ginger extended her hand.

"Mr. Fulton, how do you do?"

"Very well, Mrs. Reed. Thank you once again for this opportunity."

"It will be my pleasure, should you and Master Scout get on." It was premature for Ginger to give Scout the title, but it was only a matter of time before official adoption proceedings would begin. New laws regulating adoption were in process in England, and Ginger wanted everything to be done legally and correctly.

Mr. Fulton bobbed his head in understanding. "I shall do my best to teach and train the youngster."

"Very well," Ginger said. "Do follow me. I have the library set aside for Scout's daily instruction." Ginger led the way across the black and white marble flooring of the main entrance, which was well lit by the tall windows by day and by the grand chandelier that hung high above by night. Boss followed on Ginger's heels as she walked up the curving staircase. The hem of her chemise frock floated lightly just below her knees, a fashion trend considered rather scandalous. Never in the history of time had the female race, especially those from respectable social classes, brazenly shown so much stocking-covered leg.

The library was situated to the right of the landing, and the door was open in expectation.

"I hope this will suffice," Ginger said. The library wasn't a large room, but Ginger felt this lent it a homy and warm atmosphere. The walls were all but concealed by shelves of books; a large rug covered most of the wooden floor; a fireplace had coals glowing orange with large chairs perfect for curling up with a good book angling towards it. Under the window was a desk and chair where Scout could do his lessons.

"Indeed," Mr. Fulton said. "Learning is best done whilst surrounded by great literary works."

"I hope you'll find the shelves well stocked. If there's a volume missing that you desire for Scout's education, please do let me know, and I'll arrange for it to be obtained."

"Yes, madam."

"You may set up," Ginger said. "I'll have Scout brought to you shortly."

Scout was not to be found in his new bedroom nor anywhere on the main floor. Though Ginger had instructed him not to interfere with Mrs. Beasley in the kitchen, old habits did die hard, and Ginger headed through the green baize door to the servants' area at the back of the house.

"I'll not serve the likes of him as though he's died and woken up a bloody prince."

Ginger frowned. Mrs. Beasley was having the most difficult time adjusting to Scout's new status.

"It's not the lad's fault."

Clement was speaking this time. "It's as hard for him as it is for you."

"I highly doubt that. I don't see him preparing a four-course meal for the likes of me."

Ginger cleared her throat before stepping into view. Mrs. Beasley's round, puffy face grew redder than a beetroot.

Clement stiffened then bowed. "My apologies, madam. We weren't expecting you."

Mrs. Beasley curtsied deeply, far more than Ginger had ever seen the stout woman do. "Madam."

"I understand this situation is difficult," Ginger said, reining in her anger. The English class system was proving to be a pain in the neck. "However, I'm the mistress of Hartigan House, and things shall be run my way. If either of you has a problem with it, you can give your notice."

"No, madam," Clement said. "Please forgive us. We were out of order."

Ginger noted how Clement spoke for them both. Mrs. Beasley kept her eyes to the floor, which Ginger had to concede, was spotless.

"Very well. I am looking for Master Scout. Have either of you seen him?"

Boss barked as if conjuring the lad, and Scout walked in from outside. His eyes widened as he registered the tension in the kitchen.

"Were you looking for me, Missus Mum?"

Ginger pretended not to see the bemused glance shared by Clement and Mrs. Beasley at this new title.

"Yes, Scout." She reached out her hand. "Mr. Fulton is waiting for you in the library."

Scout took Ginger's hand with a look of reluctance. Ginger kept her chin up. She had to win these small battles if she intended to win the war. This much she'd learned in France, where she'd served during the Great War. Unlike what most people believed about her, she hadn't worked for the telephone exchange, but rather the British Secret Service, which was both an honour and a burden to bear. The things she'd witnessed and participated in during those years would forever remain secret.

Scout held back shyly as he peered at the new tutor. Ginger made quick introductions.

"Scout, this is your tutor, Mr. Fulton. Mr. Fulton, this is Scout." She bent lower to look Scout in the eye. "I expect you to show Mr. Fulton the respect he deserves, and to work hard at what ever task or exercise he asks of you."

Scout responded unenthusiastically. "Yes, Missus Mum."

Mr. Fulton stared back with a look of confidence that eased Ginger's mind. The two of them would get along just fine.

Once she'd gathered her belongings, Ginger let Pippins know she was leaving for the day. "I'm not sure when I'll be back, but Mrs. Beasley can assume that dinner with the Reeds will go ahead as planned."

CHAPTER SIX

*G*inger spent time ensuring her office was in order. Though Felicia was responsible for filing case documents, Ginger liked to make sure nothing slipped through the cracks. Once her desk was cleared, she decided a cup of tea was in order and entered the small kitchen just behind the central area. Coffee mugs made of green glass the colour of sea foam lined one open shelf and beside them stood a row of fancy teacups and their corresponding saucers. A small sink and a gas ring were on the counter along with a canister of sugar. Tucked into the stone wall was a small cool pantry for storing milk.

Ginger put the kettle on the gas ring and when the water came to a boil, filled a pot to which she had already added tea leaves. Before she had a chance to let it brew, the telephone rang in the other room. She hurried to answer it.

"Ginger, love, it's Basil."

"Basil! Is it true? Has Reginald Peck died?"

"I'm afraid he has. In fact, his body is at the mortuary here at the Yard, since the hospital is too busy to accept it. Apparently there's been a traffic accident, unfortunately."

"Is Dr. Gupta doing an autopsy?"

"Yes. Even though Mr. Peck's physician has determined his death as from natural causes, the solicitor has requested the postmortem."

"The solicitor?"

"Apparently, Mr. Peck himself made it a requirement of his will."

"How very intriguing. You don't mind if I pop in, do you, love?"

Ginger heard Basil chuckling on the end of the line. "I expected no less."

"Come on, Bossy," Ginger said as she returned the receiver. "We're going for a motorcar ride."

Ginger collected her things, put Boss on his leash, and locked up as she left. Her curiosity was most definitely ignited.

The shortest route to Scotland Yard was through Westminster on Victoria Street and then north on Whitehall. Ginger was quite perplexed as to the nature of her fellow drivers and wondered at the unreasonable honking of horns that seemed to follow her.

She patted Boss on the head before going inside. "You should stay here. I know you'd rather join me, but why not have a nice nap?"

Dr. Gupta, the pathologist at Scotland Yard, was a good doctor and a good man. Ginger had become acquainted with him when he worked at the London Medical School for Women, where Ginger's good friend Haley Higgins had once studied. Though Ginger wouldn't say she and Dr. Gupta were friends, they were colleagues who respected one another.

Basil and Dr. Gupta were conferring when Ginger stepped into the basement mortuary. Constable Braxton, Basil's accompanying officer, waited for Basil at the entrance. He was young and new to Scotland Yard, and much like Basil, had joined the force out of interest rather than financial need. Brian Braxton was pleasant-looking and charming, and, Ginger was reasonably certain, soft on Felicia.

"Good day, Constable," Ginger said with a smile.

"Good day, Mrs. Reed."

Part way through the autopsy, Dr. Gupta opened the Y incision to reveal the vital organs. Ginger didn't even blink. She'd seen Haley perform the procedure more than once, and, anyway, nothing could compare to the carnage she'd witnessed on the bloody fields in France.

"Examination of the stomach contents shows that Mr. Peck had eaten buttered toast the night before he died and had drunk a cup of tea."

"Cause of death?" Basil asked.

"Heart failure."

"He had a known condition," Basil said.

Dr. Gupta glanced up from his work. "I'm not convinced that his death was from natural causes."

"Why not?" Ginger asked.

"It's the tea in his stomach. It has an odd smell."

"Do you suspect poison?" she asked.

"It's hard to say. I'd like to run some tests as a precaution."

"Indeed," Basil said. "Please let us know as soon as the results come back."

"Naturally." Dr. Gupta made large stitches, closing the skin back in place.

To be polite, Ginger asked after his wife. "How is Mrs. Gupta?"

"She's well, thank you."

Mrs. Gupta was with child, but propriety forbade Ginger to enquire further. "Please give her my regards," Ginger added.

Dr. Gupta considered Ginger with his copper-coloured eyes, which were even more striking next to his brown skin and shiny, black, close-cropped hair. "I shall."

Basil turned, and Ginger looked to him eagerly.

"I'm heading over to Eaton Square. Care to join me, Lady Gold?"

Ginger smiled at the use of her former title, now her investigative alter ego. "I'd love to, Chief Inspector."

THE FIRST TIME Basil had allowed Ginger to assist on a case was when they'd met on board the SS *Rosa*. Initially, he'd found her insistence on "nosing in on police business" intrusive until she'd explained that a non-authoritative female presence worked in Basil's favour when conducting interviews. The suspects tended to let their guard down. She'd been proven correct in that case and others, not to mention the fact that she'd since saved Basil's life on more than one occasion.

Those in policing in the London area had become accustomed to seeing the two working together, and now that Ginger had become an official investigator in her own right, there was, with a few exceptions, even less resistance to her presence.

Eaton Square Gardens was a rectangular strip of lavish grounds. The houses, made of white stone, had two to three bays in their width and were four or five floors in height. The June climate was proving to be unseasonably warm. The sun's rays illuminated the beauty of the natural setting: birds chirping, flowers blooming, the smell of spring growth.

All in stark contrast to a dark-minded deed of murder that had occurred just behind the walls of the prestigious house belonging to the notable Peck family, Basil thought as he stood at the door with Constable Braxton on one side and Ginger on the other.

The butler answered the chiming of the doorbell.

"Good morning," Basil said. "I'm Chief Inspector Reed, and this is Constable Braxton, and my consultant, Lady Gold. We're here on police business."

The butler hesitated briefly then motioned for them to enter.

"Your name, please?" Basil asked once the door behind them had been closed.

"Murphy, sir."

"Murphy, please let Mrs. Peck know we're here."

Murphy guided them to the sitting room where Basil and Ginger shared the yellow velvet settee, and Constable Braxton stayed standing. Mrs. Peck joined them shortly afterwards, looking more fragile than Basil remembered. She lowered herself into one of the matching chairs.

Gone were the cheery spring prints of ladies' fashion. Mrs. Peck wore a black frock—stylish with a long black silk scarf around her pale neck and a black satin sash around the hips—suitable for mourning, and held a white silk handkerchief in her black-gloved hands. As expected, her mood was equally sombre.

A maid followed Mrs. Peck in with a tea tray and set it on the coffee table.

"You don't mind that I've requested tea. I need something to do with my hands."

"No, please go ahead," Basil said.

Mrs. Peck poured for the three of them but ignored Constable Braxton who was waiting by the door.

"It's a blend I have shipped in from India. You can't buy it in the shops here, but I do find it comforting at a time like this."

"Thank you," Ginger said. She took a sip and had to agree it was lovely.

"About your husband," Basil began.

Mrs. Peck's hand shook as she returned her teacup to its saucer. "I honestly can't believe he's gone. Even though his personal physician has been predicting the demise of Reginald's heart for years now, I was starting to believe he didn't know what he was speaking about. Until recently, he'd really rallied." Mrs. Peck dabbed at her eyes. "I just thought we had more time."

"I'm very sorry for your loss," Ginger offered.

Mrs. Peck relaxed at the sentiment. "Thank you,

Mrs. Reed."

"Mrs. Peck," Basil began, "I know this is difficult, but would you have any reason to believe that someone might've wanted your husband dead?"

"I'm afraid I don't understand? Are you saying—?"

"It's possible your husband may have been murdered."

Mrs. Peck's eyes widened with shock. "No, you must be mistaken. Reginald's heart just gave out. He's been ill for several years. No, what you're saying just simply can't be true!"

"I'm sorry, Mrs. Peck, but the medical examiner has reason to believe that your husband was poisoned."

Mrs. Peck covered her face with her hands and emitted a soft sob. Basil shared a look with Ginger, whose green eyes were filled with pity.

"That doesn't make sense," she finally said. "He was dying anyway. I know I just said I didn't believe the prognosis, but I suppose, if I'm honest, it's because I didn't want to believe it. It was quite obvious that he was unwell. You saw him at the gala last night. His mood was less than cordial. He was easily aggravated when he felt poorly. He went to bed early."

"Do you know if he ate or drank anything before retiring?" Basil asked.

"He usually had a piece of toast and a cup of tea."

"Who prepared it?" Ginger asked.

"Well, you'd have to ask Mrs. McCullagh, my housekeeper, about that. I suppose whichever maid was on duty last night."

"It's my understanding that you have a guest on the premises?" Basil checked his notebook. "Mr. Cyril Wilding?"

Mrs. Peck blinked. "He's a family friend, my side, you see. He has nothing to do with this except to be visiting at a bad time."

"And where's he from?"

"From?"

"Yes. He's staying with you, so I assume he's from out of town?"

"Oh, yes. Well, he's a Londoner, but without a place to stay at the moment."

Basil approached Braxton and asked him to fetch Mr. Wilding.

The young man appeared to be in his mid-twenties. He wore an expensive suit and had his hair trimmed short around the ears, and well-oiled off his smooth face with a sharp side parting. He was the type with a continuous youthful, red blush to the cheeks, and could, from a distance, be mistaken for someone much younger.

"Please have a seat," Basil said. He didn't excuse Mrs. Peck because it would have been rude to do so without cause, and she didn't leave of her own accord.

"I understand you are a guest of the Peck family," Basil said.

Wilding was quick to correct him. "I'm a friend of Mrs. Peck's."

"I see. And how long have you been staying here?"

Wilding glanced at Mrs. Peck and then said, "Three weeks, give or take a day or so."

"How well did you know Mr. Reginald Peck?" Ginger asked.

"Not at all."

Mrs. Peck interjected. "Cyril and I go back a long way, but we lost touch, you could say. I hadn't had the opportunity to introduce him to Reginald and the others before now. So, you see, he couldn't have possibly had any reason to . . . do this terrible thing."

Wilding narrowed his eyes in confusion. "What terrible thing? Wait? You're not say—"

Basil cut him off. "I'm afraid we have reason to suspect that Mr. Peck's death may be suspicious in nature."

"How unfortunate." Wilding was quick to add, "I didn't even know Mr. Peck, and I certainly had nothing to hold against him."

Basil thought him rather fast to defend against any possible motives but kept that to himself.

"Thank you, Mrs. Peck and Mr. Wilding. That will be all for now."

CHAPTER SEVEN

*M*rs. McCullagh was preoccupied on the telephone making orders for the kitchen, so Basil called on the scullery maid. He'd decided he might as well start from the bottom of the staffing ladder.

The young girl sat shyly on a chair in the breakfast room. She cast furtive glances towards Braxton that resulted in a red flushing of her cheeks. Basil couldn't say if Braxton's presence was helpful in these situations, but he couldn't very well dismiss the man for being handsome.

"Constable," Basil said, pulling the officer to the side.

"Yes, sir."

Basil lowered his voice. "Have a wander about the

house, but be discreet. Keep an eye and ear out for anything that might be out of the ordinary.

"Yes, sir."

Once Braxton had gone, Basil took a seat beside Ginger at the table.

"I'm Chief Inspector Reed," he said, "and this is my consultant, Lady Gold."

The maid kept her chin down and eyes averted. "Sir, madam."

"Please state your name," Basil said. "For the record."

"Daisy Peele."

"How long have you worked for Mr. and Mrs. Peck?"

"Only a month, sir."

New to the household. Did she have a connection to the deceased? Basil wondered. In order for her to have easy access to Mr. Peck, had someone arranged for her employ?

"How did you come about your employment here?"

"It was on Lady Clifford's recommendation that Mrs. McCullagh took me on, sir."

"Scullery maid?"

"Yes, sir."

"And your duties as such?" Basil knew the conventional tasks assigned to the lowest rung, but he wanted to get Daisy used to speaking aloud.

"I clean the fireplaces and start the fires in the mornings, scrub the floors, wash the dishes, and other such things. Most of my time is spent in the kitchen with the cook."

Basil referred to his notes. "Mrs. Johnson?"

"That's right, sir."

"Did you work for Lord and Lady Clifford?" Ginger asked.

Daisy nodded. "Two years. Then they—"

"Yes?" Ginger prompted.

"I shouldn't speak out of turn, madam."

Ginger smiled. "It's okay, Daisy, when it's a detective asking the questions."

Daisy seemed to relax. Basil held in a grin. Ginger had a way of making his suspects loosen up.

"All right, then," Daisy started. "Apparently, they came into money troubles. I weren't the only one let go."

"I see." Basil made a note to enquire at the neighbours', just as a matter of form. Then to Daisy he said, "Did you take Mr. Peck his evening tea last night?"

Daisy shook her head. "No, sir. It's not my place to mix with those above."

Basil wanted to speak to Mrs. Johnson, the cook, but

since midday was upon them, she was busy making the luncheon. Mrs. McCullagh sent in Josie Roth, the parlour maid, with a promise to be next, but that Josie was needed and would Basil mind hurrying things along.

Josie was petite yet not weak in appearance. Her hair was fashionably short but tucked under a white maid's cap.

"How long have you been in Mr. Peck's employ?" Basil asked.

"Eight years, sir."

"Since he and Mrs. Peck were married?"

"Yes, sir."

"Did you take Mr. Peck his evening tea last night?"

"No, sir. Mr. Murphy usually took care of that."

Basil jotted the information about the butler in his notepad.

"Was Mr. Peck difficult to work for?" From what Basil had witnessed of the man, he wasn't surprised by Josie's reluctance to answer.

"It's okay," Ginger said. "What you say to us is in the strictest confidence."

"Not very easy, sir."

"Was there anyone in this household who held a grudge against Mr. Peck?"

"Oh, sir, I really wouldn't know. Below stairs don't mix with those above much."

"But as the parlour maid, you must hear or see

things?" Basil knew that maids were often treated as if they were invisible by those "above", except, of course, when things were wanted.

Josie stiffened. "I mind my own business, sir."

"Josie," Ginger said kindly. "It's your duty to cooperate with the police."

"Yes, madam. Forgive me, sir. The members of the Peck family don't get along so well. There's a lot of arguing, but I think, for some, that's just the way they do things. It don't make them bad people."

THE NEXT PERSON TO sit before them was the cook, a tall, red-faced lady with chubby arms crossing a rather ample bosom. A scowl etched her doughy face.

"I'm very busy, y'know. I only just got lunch out, and I've got to start preparing the evening meal. What is it that you got to do with me?"

"Mrs. Johnson, you are aware that Mr. Peck has passed away?" Basil said.

"Of course I am. It's why I'm busy. There's much to do when there's a funeral to cater for."

Basil shared a look with Ginger and let out a short breath. "I'll do my best to be brief. How long have you been employed here?"

"Six years this July. I remember because of Peace Day."

"Ah, yes," Ginger said. Peace Day was the British bank holiday marking the end of the Great War.

"Do you like your work here?" Basil asked.

Mrs. Johnson shifted a thick shoulder. "It's a position."

"Do you ever have problems with rodents?" Ginger asked.

Basil glanced at his wife. Rat poison was always a possibility in poison deaths.

Mrs. Johnson looked like a duck whose feathers had been ruffled. "My kitchen is kept clean to the highest possible standards, I can assure you."

"I meant no offence," Ginger said. "A rodent problem can be found in any establishment. Even Buckingham Palace, I'm sure. The intelligent thing to do in such a situation would be to treat the matter immediately."

"We don't have a rat problem," Mrs. Johnson insisted, "but if we did, I do keep a jar of strychnine on hand to eliminate the little beasts immediately."

"Did you have any interaction with Mr. Peck?" Basil asked.

"I stay below stairs for the most part."

She paused, then lowered her voice. "If you're looking into the past of the family members, you might find something less than perfect under Mrs. Peck's carpet."

"Like what?"

"It's only gossip, mind, and I don't really know the details. It's just what I've heard."

"Thank you, Mrs. Johnson," Basil said. "You may go."

Mrs. Johnson bobbed and scurried away like the furry creatures in question.

"What do you think?" Ginger asked.

Basil furrowed his brow in thought. "I fail to see a motive, but she obviously doesn't esteem Mrs. Peck enough to worry about her reputation. I'll get Braxton to do a background search on the staff to see if there are any past connections we don't know about."

Murphy stepped into the room. "Forgive my intrusion, Chief Inspector, but you have a telephone call."

The butler led him to the telephone room then gave him privacy as he answered.

"Chief Inspector Reed, here."

"Hello, Chief Inspector."

Basil recognised the voice of the medical examiner.

"Hello, Dr. Gupta."

"Test results have come in. I—"

"Please wait, Doctor." Basil didn't want to risk being overheard, and he wouldn't put it past the family members or staff to be listening in, not to mention the possibility of an unethical telephone operator. "I'll come to you."

CHAPTER EIGHT

*I*t was a good time to break from the Pecks as luncheon was being taken. Without a good cause to intrude, it would be less than prudent for the reputation of Scotland Yard to be found insensitive and intrusive, especially when dealing with such a prominent family. Ginger returned to her office on Watson Street, intending to check on matters at Feathers & Flair. Basil had promised to ring once he had more information. Boss needed a walk and was happy to go on a short stroll to the dress shop around the corner.

The Regent Street shop had the elegance required of a fashion salon: marble floors, high ceilings moulded in gold and dotted with electric chandeliers. The main floor flaunted the designs of all the top designers in the industry, whilst the upper level hosted the tremendously popular factory-made frocks.

Madame Roux, the shop manager, finished a dress order at the sales desk and then waved the customer off. "Thank you, Mrs. Courtney. We'll ring you when your gown eez ready!"

Ginger nodded at the happy customer as she passed. "Good day, Mrs. Courtney."

Mrs. Courtney tapped Ginger's arm. "Your designs are outstanding, Mrs. Reed. You have a bright mind in your fashion designer student, Emma."

"Thank you, Mrs. Courtney. I'm thrilled you liked them."

Ginger smiled at her beaming shop manager and stated the obvious. "The salon appointment went well."

"*Bien, bien*, Mrs. Reed. And the new girl, Miss Tatum, was a big success in the salon and dramatised Emma's creations for Mrs. Courtney."

Millie Tatum was Ginger's newest employee. Ginger wanted to compete with the London salons, and so had had a special fitting room designed for clients. It was Millie's job to model original designs Ginger and Emma had worked on together.

"Fabulous," Ginger said. She released Boss from his leash, and he made his way to his bed behind the velvet curtain. "I'm relieved to hear that Miss Tatum has turned out well."

"She's not much for personality," Madame Roux said, "but her figure eez divine."

"Is she still here?" Ginger worried that the young girl might've overheard and didn't want her to have reason to feel offended.

"No, no," Madame Roux said. "I let her go home now that our final client has left."

Ginger found her seamstress, Emma, in the back room; she sewed madly on the new Vickers sewing machine. Leaning her head over her work, her eyes focused on the needle, and her foot worked the treadle.

"Emma," Ginger said. "You are to be congratulated. Mrs. Courtney loved your work."

"They're designs we've created together, Mrs. Reed. I admit it was very gratifying to have them so quickly appreciated."

"Madame Roux says Millie did a fine job modelling."

"She did, madam." Emma flashed a smile then returned to her creation.

"Don't work too late," Ginger admonished. "I need you to be fresh in the morning."

"Yes, madam," Emma said without looking up.

Ginger chuckled and felt satisfied with her lot in life. Feathers & Flair was doing well, and Ginger's staff pleased her, including, she thought pleasantly, Dorothy West, who'd once given her a moment of concern. Over time, the shop assistant had grown competent at running the second floor where the factory frocks were on display. It was the younger lot, much like Dorothy, who ran with this new trend in affordable and accessible fashion.

Ginger checked on the new factory frocks and gave Dorothy instructions on how to best display them. She reviewed designs with Emma and went over prestigious client schedules with Madame Roux—with the promise to be present for the more demanding clients. Once Ginger was satisfied that everything was running smoothly, she returned with Boss to the office on Watson Street in anticipation of Felicia's return. Whatever had happened to her? Surely, the task hadn't taken this long?

As she waited, Ginger felt a little sympathy for Felicia's sense of restlessness. One could only tidy up one's desk so much before one's entire time was spent watching the telephone and wishing for it to ring.

Boss, who was curled up on her lap, whimpered and stared up with his deep dark eyes.

"Did I wake you with my fidgeting?" Ginger asked. She stroked her pet, and he pressed his head into her palm. He closed his eyes, his mouth in that perpetual smile that transmitted forgiveness.

When the telephone did ring, Ginger startled, then lifted the cradle receiver to her ear.

"Lady Gold Investigations."

"Ginger, it's me, Felicia. I'm calling from a telephone box on Russell Square."

Ginger knew of the location. The white telephone box with a red door was as tall and wide as it needed to be to accommodate one large man who might desire to make or receive a call whilst away from the convenience of his home or place of business.

"Yes, Felicia? What have you found out?"

"The sister went to work at the curiosity shop just as she had said." Ginger noted the hint of disgust in her voice. "A call to her employer would've cleared things up for him, wouldn't it? Why go to the bother of getting us to do it for him?"

"He mightn't have trusted the lady in charge. It's not unheard of for one woman to lie for another."

"Yes, I suppose you are right."

"Are you coming back soon? Boss needs a walk, and I don't want to close the office prematurely."

"I guess so." Felicia sighed. "My book won't write itself."

"That's the spirit."

Ginger had only just hung up when the instrument rang again.

"When it rains, it pours, Bossy, doesn't it?"

She lifted the receiver. "Regent 3205. Lady Gold Investigations."

"Ginger, it's Basil."

Ginger straightened at the sound of her husband's authoritative voice.

"Yes?"

"I'm at the mortuary with Dr. Gupta."

"What have you learned?"

"Mr. Peck's cause of death was poisoning. The doctor assures me the heart incident was a result of that and not natural causes."

"Rat poison?" Ginger asked.

"The type of poison is yet to be determined."

"Josie said Mr. Murphy took Mr. Peck his tea," Ginger said.

"Indeed, but I doubt he would've prepared it. It could've been anyone who had access to the kitchen."

"That would be every family member and all the staff."

"I'm heading back to Eaton Square now to continue the interviews."

"I'll meet you there."

"Very good."

Ginger hung up and stared at the office door. Felicia should be back any minute. Ginger didn't like leaving the office closed so much, but at times, it couldn't be helped. She collected her things and took a moment in front of the mirror to apply a fresh layer of lipstick and to pin on her hat. Then she donned her summer gloves and grabbed her handbag.

She stared down at Boss. "What to do with you? If you come with me, you'll have to wait in the Crossley."

Boss sat obediently, but his stub of a tail wagged against the floor. Ginger could tell he was eager for the motorcar ride and didn't mind one bit if he was left in it to take a nap.

"Very well, let's go."

Her aggravation at closing the office during the day was alleviated when a black taxicab pulled to a stop at the kerb, and Felicia appeared.

"Good timing!" Ginger said.

Felicia eyed Ginger suspiciously. "Where are you off to?"

"I'm consulting with Basil on the Peck murder case. I've only just locked up. Do you have your key?"

"I do. Did you want me to take Boss?"

Ginger looked at Boss' hopeful face then shook her head. "No, he can come with me."

The drive through Mayfair and past the Ritz Hotel along the north end of Green Park was pleasant, though she had to hold her tongue as the motor vehicles and horse-drawn carriages carelessly vied for room on the roads. Soon, she was in the district of Belgravia and on Eaton Square.

A police vehicle was parked in front of the Peck house, and Ginger pulled her Crossley up behind it.

She greeted Basil with a kiss. They were newly-weds, after all. "I know we've only been parted a couple of hours, but I'm always happy to see you."

Basil grabbed her by the wrist, then pushed her back. "No. We must stay professional." He glanced at Constable Braxton who had the good manners to look away. He whispered into her ear. "But by gosh, Ginger, you are a temptation!"

Ginger laughed, and Boss barked.

CHAPTER NINE

*O*nce they were admitted to the Pecks' house, Basil immediately arranged for the family to be gathered.

Matthew Peck was the first to protest. "What is the meaning of this? Don't you have any respect for those in mourning?"

"I do apologise," Basil said, "but I'm afraid I have disturbing news. The medical examiner has concluded that Mr. Reginald Peck was murdered."

His announcement was followed by gasps of surprise and horror. Basil carefully watched the group for signs of anyone who might not be shocked by his words, but no one stood out. If the killer was in this room, he or she was very clever, and capable of concealment.

A sob came from Deirdre Northcott. She had a

handkerchief at the ready and sniffed into it. "Oh, poor Daddy."

"Are you certain?" Mrs. Peck asked. "You're not speculating as before?"

"I'm afraid it's been confirmed, Mrs. Peck," Basil said.

"What is she here for?" Matthew Peck sneered in Ginger's direction. "We don't need spectators. Let our family grieve in peace."

"I'm here with my officer, Constable Braxton, and my consultant, Lady Gold, an acclaimed private detective. They will be assisting me with my interviews."

Deirdre Northcott narrowed her gaze onto Ginger. "I've heard of you," she said with interest. "I'm a believer in rights for the female gender and follow stories regarding the work of strong women in the city. What you've accomplished, Lady Gold, is admirable."

Ginger smiled with appreciation. "Thank you, Mrs. Northcott."

"Surely you don't suspect any of us?" This was from Mrs. Northcott's husband, Mr. Alastair Northcott, who had arrived wearing a garment made of golden thread resembling something British people would wear to bed. Basil had learned the night before that he preferred to be addressed as Arjun. Basil didn't comply.

"Mr. Northcott, the nature of Mr. Peck's demise

points to the likelihood of a crime being committed by someone who had regular contact with him, which includes everyone in this room." He turned to Mrs. Peck. "So that you can get on with your tasks for the day, which I'm sure are many, we can perhaps, start with you, madam?"

Mrs. Peck lowered her chin indicating consent.

To the room, he pronounced, "No one is to leave the premises until after they have been interviewed. Constable Braxton will stay with you."

The interviews took place in the drawing room which was decorated with rich, dark wooden furnishes, items trimmed with gold, and an impressive electric chandelier.

Basil and Ginger sat on the luxurious settee.

"Do you mind if I ring for a cup of tea?" Mrs. Peck said. "My throat is parched from sorrow."

"Of course not," Basil said.

Mrs. Peck pulled on the rope of the bell before taking a chair. Josie scurried in shortly afterwards.

"Madam?" she said with a curtsy.

"Tea, Josie, please."

"Yes, madam."

"This is such a dreadful affair," Ginger said kindly. "You must be shattered."

"I am." Mrs. Peck's eyes grew glassy with tears. "I knew the day was coming, of course, but I thought we had a little more time. Now, to hear my dear Reginald's life was most certainly cut short—" She blew into the lace handkerchief crumpled in her fist.

"Can you tell me about your husband's illness?" Basil asked.

"I've been told he had a weak heart," Mrs. Peck replied. "Apparently, he'd been born with it. I told him he should give up his businesses, that the stress of running them would kill him, but he wouldn't listen to me. Oh, why'd he have to be so headstrong?"

Quiet as a mouse, Josie slid a tea tray with a porcelain teapot and three cups and saucers onto the table.

"Can I interest you in a cup?" Mrs. Peck said. "It's my favourite blend, once again."

Ginger took Mrs. Peck up on her offer. Basil didn't take to the flavour, and so declined. He preferred a regular cup of Earl Grey.

Ginger, on the other hand, seemed to rather like it. "This is quite good, Mrs. Peck. I must get the name of your importer."

Mrs. Peck glanced back wryly. "I'll see to it." The way she said it, Basil somehow doubted she would. A lady like Mrs. Peck might like to keep her special things to herself.

Like all the rooms, the drawing room had large flourishing potted plants.

"Is botany a passion of yours?" Ginger asked.

Mrs. Peck's hand trembled as she returned her teacup to its saucer. "No, that was all Reginald. Even up to his dying day, he took care of his flowers upstairs. He was especially fond of the exotic kinds."

"You have a lift that goes to the roof?" Basil asked.

"I believe Reginald lived for the hours he spent there," Mrs. Peck said after a sip of tea.

"There seem to be a lot of plants to care for," Ginger said.

Mrs. Peck chuckled dryly. "I sometimes feel like I live in a conservatory. Murphy was a big help to Reginald in that regard."

"I see. Would you say that Mr. Murphy was a confidant of your husband's?" Basil asked.

Mrs. Peck stiffened. "Mr. Peck and I *were* happily married, Chief Inspector. He confided in *me*. There were no secrets between us. Neither of us would have considered the possibility of confiding in someone in our employ. And if he needed a male confidant, I suspect his valet, Barlow, would've been a preferred choice."

"No offence intended, Mrs. Peck," Basil said. "Am I correct in stating that you are Mr. Peck's second wife and that Mr. Matthew Peck and Mrs. Deirdre North-cott are your stepchildren?"

"That is correct. Reginald's first wife passed away ten years ago. A dreadful equine accident."

"And you've been married to Mr. Peck for how long?"

Mrs. Peck blinked, then said, "Eight and a half years."

Basil and Ginger shared a brief look. Mrs. Peck was quick in her defence. "Margaret and I were friends, and I'd often visit. Reginald would join us in our conversation. There was nothing untoward between us whilst Margaret was alive, though he confessed to me later that his marriage to Margaret had been a lonely time for him."

"I see," Basil said, as he jotted a short note.

Ginger then appealed to Mrs. Peck. "I know this must be so difficult for you to consider, but who do you think would want to see your husband dead?"

"In my household? No one! Everyone under this roof knew it was only a matter of time for Reginald. It just doesn't make sense."

"Indeed not," Basil said, "yet, that very thing happened."

"Perhaps someone broke in without our knowledge, or perhaps hid in the house after the party. He had work associates. You might call on them."

"Who in particular?" Basil asked.

"Well, I'm not all that sure, Chief Inspector. I had absolutely nothing to do with Reginald's business affairs, but you might start with his secretary, Mr. Ryerson. Reginald had become quite agitated with him by the end."

CHAPTER TEN

Ginger couldn't help but feel pity for Mrs.
Peck. To lose one's husband was traumatic
enough, as Ginger well knew, but to have his
death be ruled a murder would tremendously heighten
the burden.

Matthew Peck claimed his stepmother's empty
seat. The young man looked to be in his late twenties,
well dressed in a pinstripe suit, a silk bow tie, and
patent leather shoes. The wrinkles on his forehead
belied his age, and his dark-eyed gaze appeared
haunted. He carried his arm as if it pained him. His
knee jiggled with nerves, and his good hand slapped at
it, causing it to still.

"I understand you served in the war," Basil said.

"Like most men still living, sir," Mr. Peck said. "I
assume you were there as well?"

"Yes."

Basil's answer was short. Ginger knew he didn't like to dwell on how an early injury had invalided him out of fighting whilst the war was still in its infancy.

"Took a bullet in your arm, then?" Basil asked.

"At least I still have it, as useless as it is."

"Quite right," Basil said. "Now, what can you tell me about your father?"

"Father was ill," Mr. Peck said. "Are you sure your 'expert doctor' hasn't got his diagnosis mixed up?"

"Quite certain," Basil said. "Did the two of you get on?"

Mr. Peck lifted his good shoulder. "We didn't see eye to eye, you could say. He was frightfully old fashioned in his thinking. Especially—" Matthew shrugged. "Well, he was a crafty brute underneath his fine suits and silk cravats."

"Especially?" Ginger prodded.

"Sorry?"

"You were saying that your father was old-fashioned in his thinking," Ginger said with a batting of her eyelashes. She'd learned that unexpected signs of flirtation could throw a gentleman enough to let the truth slip out. "But didn't complete your thought."

"Yes, quite. Father hung on to old ideas regarding money. He trusted the banks and invested conservatively in the stock market, whilst I encouraged more dramatic investments. He would say silly things like 'Slow and steady wins the race. Don't forget the tortoise and the hare!' Those are stories for infants, I say. In today's world, the stock market is where fortunes are made."

"It's my understanding that your family is already in possession of a fortune," Basil said.

"Well, Father was the rich one. He wouldn't release my inheritance to me before he died, even though he was close to leaving this world. I know it sounds bad now with his death being considered suspicious."

"Indeed, Mr. Peck," Basil said. "It's motive."

"That's why I'm telling you it looks bad. I only wanted to get started on building my own fortune, but I wouldn't kill my own father to do it. I'm not a monster."

"You and Mr. Northcott were in a heated argument last night," Basil stated.

Mr. Peck's focus darted about the room. "Family members argue."

"What was the nature of your argument?"

"I don't see how that is relevant."

"This is a murder investigation, Mr. Peck. Please answer the question."

"Very well. Northcott or *Arjun*, as he ridiculously insists on being called, likes to boast about making a vow to a simpler life. In actuality, he lost his money on bad investments and moved to India because it's a place in the empire where one can live like a rich man with little means. He simply can't stand that I was about to inherit."

"Would your sister, Mrs. Northcott, not also inherit?" Ginger asked. As yet, no one had been made aware of the contents of Mr. Peck's will.

"Deirdre chose Northcott against Father's wishes. He threatened to cut her out of his will if she married him."

"And did he?" Basil asked.

"He never said either way."

Basil released Mr. Peck with the request that Mr. Northcott be brought in.

"What do you think?" Ginger asked when they were alone.

"He has motive and opportunity," Basil said. "Quite jumpy. I'd say he suffers somewhat from shell shock. A man can lose his mind that way."

"Enough to turn him into a murderer?" Ginger asked.

"Stranger things have happened. Once we know for certain the nature of the poison used, perhaps we'll be able to determine means."

. . .

No MATTER HIS ethnic dress or change of name, Mr. Alastair Northcott had a hard time pulling off the essence of what was Indian, Ginger thought. His skin was too pale and his hair too blond. And you couldn't have a more British-sounding name than Northcott.

Despite this, Mr. Northcott placed two palms together in front of his chest and bowed. "*Namaste.*"

"Please be seated, Mr. Northcott," Basil said.

"I prefer Arjun, please."

Basil straightened his shoulders and exhaled. "Because of the nature of these interviews, we'll have to stay with our legal names." As a courtesy, he added, "I hope you don't mind."

"Whatever it takes to please the crown," Mr. Northcott responded snidely.

"I take it you and Mrs. Northcott were recently residing in India."

"That's correct."

"How long have you been living in London?"

"Five months."

Ginger smiled warmly at Mr. Northcott. "India seems like such a marvellous place. I've never been there."

Mr. Northcott's eyes sparkled in apparent pleasure. "You definitely should go sometime, Mrs. Reed. I highly recommend it. So good for one's spiritual experience."

"And what brought you back to London?" Ginger asked.

"Deirdre insisted. She heard that her father was ill. I couldn't deny her wishes to return, and I most certainly wouldn't let her travel alone."

"What were you and Mr. Matthew Peck arguing about last night?" Basil asked.

"The only thing that's ever on Matthew's mind. Money. Honestly, I wouldn't put it past the blighter to knock off his old man to stuff his pockets with more filthy mammon."

"His father was dying from his disease anyway," Ginger said. "Why risk a murder charge?"

Mr. Northcott scoffed. "The bloke is crackers and doesn't have an ounce of patience. And he's so entitled that the idea he'd get pinched for committing a crime is probably a foreign thought."

"You don't think very highly of your brother-in-law," Ginger said.

"It doesn't matter much now. One shouldn't commit murder. It's bad karma. Matthew will get what's coming to him."

Ginger and Basil exchanged wide-eyed looks of shock which weren't missed by Mr. Northcott. "Oh my, I shouldn't have said that now, should I? If something does happen to Matthew, I go on the record stating that I had nothing to do with it. I'm not a killer."

"Someone in this house is," Basil said.

"It isn't me."

"Do you and Mrs. Northcott share the same bedroom?" Basil asked.

"What? Yes, not that it's any of your business."

"So, when we call on her next, she'll tell us that you spent the whole night with her, not getting up to wander off?"

"I should hope so."

"Did she stay in bed the entire night?" Ginger asked.

"Steady on, now. Deirdre had nothing to do with her father's death."

"Answer the question, Mr. Northcott," Basil insisted.

"How should I know? I *was* sleeping. I suppose I did hear her get up to use the loo. It's habitual with her."

"What do you do for employment, Mr. Northcott?" Basil asked.

"I import goods from India and sell them to novelty shops and tea shops here in London. Like you, Mrs. Reed, many Brits have never been to the outer regions of the empire. These items provide a vicarious way to add an exotic flavour to their grey humdrum world."

"I understand that your wife was to be cut out of the will," Basil said, "as a result of her marriage to you."

Mr. Northcott sniggered. "I told her she should send me away, but alas, young love. She never thought her father would go through with his threat anyway."

"Did Mr. Reginald Peck ever say otherwise?" Ginger said. "To you."

"The old man didn't say two words to me if he could help it." Mr. Northcott picked at a piece of fuzz on his silk *kurta*. "And I wouldn't have had it any other way."

"In one breath," Ginger began, once Alastair Northcott had left the drawing room, "Mr. Northcott insists that he slept through the night, and in the next, injures his wife's alibi by saying he heard her get up."

Basil agreed. "He can't have both been soundly sleeping and also aware enough to notice that."

Deirdre Northcott arrived in Constable Braxton's company. Basil had told him to keep the married couple apart until after the interviews had taken place.

"Your stepmother left a pot of tea," Ginger said.

"Virginia's special blend, I assume?" Deirdre said. "Nasty stuff. I'll pass."

Basil got straight to the point. "I understand that you were cut out of your father's will."

"So he said."

"But you didn't believe him?" Ginger asked.

"I preferred to keep our conversations civil, which meant staying away from certain subjects. Money and my husband were the top two offenders."

"Someone in this household murdered your father."

"It could've been anyone present at the gala," Mrs. Northcott said. "Including yourselves, I might add. Your questions to my family are futile as well as offensive."

Ginger had considered this problem before; however, not everyone prepared and delivered Mr. Peck's tea and toast.

"It's simply procedure to begin with the family first," Basil said. "Is there someone, besides us, who was at the gala last night that you suspect may have wished your father harm?"

"I can't think of anyone."

"Who had the most to gain by his death?" Ginger asked.

For the first time, fear flashed behind Mrs. Northcott's eyes. "I suppose it depends on Papa's will."

"Matthew?" Basil asked.

Mrs. Northcott's eyes narrowed darkly. "Matthew had nothing to do with this!"

"Perhaps yourself then," Basil said.

"I had the least to gain by his death. He promised

to cut me out of his will remember, which gives me no motive to end my father's life."

"Unless he hadn't got around to it yet," Ginger said.

"And how would I know that?"

Ginger inclined her head. "Information can be obtained if one knows how to go about it."

Deirdre pursed her lips, which Ginger noted were well drawn out and painted in the shape of a small bow.

"I know nothing about those sorts of affairs."

"Why did you and Mr. Northcott return to London?" Basil asked.

"Because I couldn't bear India. I threatened to leave my husband if we didn't leave that wretched place immediately."

"You didn't return for your father's sake?" Ginger said. "Knowing how ill he'd become?"

"That was a coincidence, one Alastair uses to excuse our departure from India."

"Mr. Peck didn't approve of your marriage to Mr. Northcott, did he?"

"I assume Matthew told you that?" Mrs. Northcott said. "Well, it's true. Life in this perfect house is definitely not perfect."

"Yet, you plan to stay?"

"Even if Papa cut me out of his will, he wouldn't

allow me to live on the streets. Despite Virginia's displeasure at the thought, I have every right to live here. More than she does. I grew up here. She's only lived here for eight years."

"To your recollection, did Mr. Northcott leave your bedroom at any time during the night?" Basil asked.

Deirdre Northcott blinked as the insinuation dawned. "Mr. Northcott likes to think he's obtained some kind of spiritual enlightenment, but in truth, he is a restless man. He often arises at an ungodly hour to meditate, even though he knows I dislike it. A pagan ritual, if you ask me."

"Did he rise to meditate last night?" Ginger asked.

Deirdre Northcott looked Ginger straight in the eye. "I do believe he did."

CHAPTER ELEVEN

The sign in the window of the solicitors' firm in Knightsbridge said Sherwood, Winthrop, and McGraw, Barristers and Solicitors. The wooden door swung open, and Mr. Laurence Winthrop himself barrelled out, nearly knocking into Ginger and Basil.

Ginger recognised the man from the gala the night before. He had a long, serious face with dark sideburns, and instead of a top hat, he now wore a grey bowler.

Basil held out his police identification card and stopped the busy man in his tracks. "Mr. Winthrop?" he said. "I'm Chief Inspector Reed of Scotland Yard, and this is my consultant, Lady Gold. Could we have a word?"

"I'm rather in a hurry, but if you don't mind walking with me. I'd like to get to the post office before it closes. It's an errand I'm obligated to do myself, I'm afraid."

Ginger shrugged in Basil's direction. Basil took the spot beside the solicitor, and since the pavement was only wide enough for two people, Ginger fell in behind.

Mr. Winthrop was built with a long torso and shorter legs, which he compensated for with a quick stride.

"Can you tell me what you and your client argued about last night at the gala?" Basil asked.

"I cannot," Mr. Winthrop said firmly. "It's privileged information."

"This is a murder investigation."

Mr. Winthrop stopped suddenly. "Murder?"

He turned to face Basil, and Ginger noted how the studious man had grown pale.

"I-I thought his heart had given out," he stammered. "It was expected it would fail one day with his condition."

Basil kept in stride. "The forensic pathologist's reports say otherwise."

Mr. Winthrop resumed his short-striding walk. "I'm sorry to hear that. But unfortunately, I can't betray confidences, even posthumously, not without a directive from a judge."

"Perhaps there are other types of questions we could ask," Ginger said from behind.

Mr. Winthrop cast her a disinterested glance. "You may try."

"How long have you been working in Mr. Peck's employ?" Ginger asked.

"Twenty years."

"After so much time," Basil started, "did you come to consider Mr. Peck a personal friend?"

"Some clients do become friendly, and some do not," was all Mr. Winthrop would concede.

Basil pressed. "And did Mr. Peck?"

Mr. Winthrop sighed. "Perhaps in the beginning, when we were younger, but life has a way of changing things for everyone. When Mr. Peck's illness took hold, he became reclusive. I was summoned for business only."

"Surely, business itself wouldn't be cause for a row?" Ginger asked.

"Some clients ask more from their solicitors than they should, Mrs. Reed."

Obviously, Mr. Winthrop knew who she was. For such a large city, London could feel rather small.

"You must be acquainted with Mr. Peck's business associates?" Basil said. "What do you know about his secretary, Mr. Ryerson?"

"Mr. Ryerson is a capable man and loyal to Mr. Peck."

"Loyalty doesn't always translate to affability."

"I believe in this case, it does."

"Who benefits from Mr. Peck's death?" Ginger asked. "One would gather Mr. Matthew Peck would have the most to gain, as the first-born son?"

Mr. Winthrop gave them a crumb. "Matthew Peck was a nuisance who hounded Mr. Peck until the end. That said, I can't comment on the contents of the will. You'll have to wait like everyone else."

They came to a halt in front of the post office. Mr. Winthrop held a small rectangular package in his hand. Ginger tried to see who the parcel was to, but Mr. Winthrop had carefully concealed the address.

"I'm afraid we must part ways," the solicitor said. "If you need me further, please make an appointment with my secretary."

MR. PECK KEPT an office in a commercial building on Fleet Street near where most of the newspaper companies were located. Ginger and Basil took the marble steps up to the offices of Peck Properties that encompassed the whole of the second floor.

They made enquiries at the receptionist's desk.

"Is Mr. Ryerson available?" Basil asked.

"Did you have an appointment?"

Basil showed the clerk his police identification card. "I'm Chief Inspector Reed. Please let Mr. Ryerson know I'm here and need to see him. It's a matter of importance."

"It's about Mr. Peck, is it?" The clerk said, his countenance darkening. "We're all simply shattered." The clerk ducked his chin then disappeared behind a closed door.

"Mr. Peck has spared no expense in keeping his offices up to date," Ginger said. She admired the modern art deco wallpaper and noticed the quality of the furniture in the waiting area.

The clerk returned shortly. "Please follow me, Chief Inspector."

For a one-and-a-quarter-million-pound enterprise, Ginger had expected a more frenetic atmosphere—employees with worried faces and urgent strides, but the opposite seemed true.

Mr. Ryerson was a wiry man with a severe face and an upturned nose that was well suited to keeping his pince-nez spectacles in place.

Basil removed his hat. "I'm Chief Inspector Reed, and this is Lady Gold, my consultant."

"Please, come in and have a seat," Mr. Ryerson said. "This is such a dreadful business, with Mr. Peck passing away. Of course, we knew his health was declining, but I'm afraid we're still in shock at his parting from us."

Ginger and Basil took the proffered seats. Mr. Ryerson's office was spacious and, like the rest of the surroundings Ginger had witnessed, nicely outfitted.

Mr. Ryerson threaded his fingers together and leaned over his desk, looking rather eager. "How can I help you, Chief Inspector?"

"I understand that you were Mr. Peck's personal secretary?"

"That's right, but my duties penetrate every administrative department of Peck Properties."

"How long have you worked for Mr. Peck?"

"Oh, I dare say, going on twenty years."

"Did you and Mr. Peck get on?"

Mr. Ryerson frowned. "I'd say so. Why? What's this about?"

"I'm afraid, Mr. Ryerson," Basil said, "that Mr. Peck was murdered."

Ginger watched as the secretary's face blanched to a ghoulish white. He pushed away from his desk and fell back in his chair.

"I, er, that is preposterous. I just can't believe someone would do such a thing to Mr. Peck."

"Why is that?" Ginger said. "Surely a man of Mr. Peck's influence would have enemies?"

"I suppose so, but not in this company, I assure

you. Mr. Peck treats, er, treated his employees very well. We're all quite devoted to him, you see."

Ginger looked at Basil and shared his sense of surprise. It would seem that Mr. Peck had been better at managing his business affairs than his family.

"Were you in attendance at the gala hosted by Mrs. Peck last evening?" Basil asked.

Mr. Ryerson shook his head. "Mr. Peck didn't even bother to let us know it was happening. Mrs. Peck entertained often. I believe Mr. Peck felt he was doing us all a favour by not forcing personal obligations on us."

Ginger hadn't seen Mr. Ryerson there, and so far, didn't recognise any of the faces of the people working at Peck Properties.

"According to Mrs. Peck, Mr. Peck had become agitated with you."

"I dare say it wasn't with me alone. In the last couple of weeks, it was as if he had had a personality change. I guessed that he was unhappy at home, but Mr. Peck never spoke to me about his personal life."

Ginger found it interesting that Mrs. Peck cast a shadow on the secretary, and he, in turn, did the same to her.

"What's going to happen to the company now?" Ginger asked.

"We don't really know. Mr. Winthrop, Mr. Peck's

solicitor, has been quite tight-lipped. I fear it will fall into Mr. Matthew Peck's hands. We're all rather worried."

"And why is that?" Basil asked.

Mr. Ryerson shifted uncomfortably. "I fear the younger Mr. Peck hasn't inherited his father's aptitude for business. And since the war, and its effects on him, I don't think the employees here will get on with him well at all."

CHAPTER TWELVE

Ginger and Basil stopped at a nearby eatery to indulge in plates of freshly fried fish and chips and sip the new American craze beverage called Coca Cola. Lunch had been a while ago and dinner with the Reeds was still several hours away.

Basil turned his nose up after taking his first gulp. "I'm not sure I like this."

"The bubbles take a bit of getting used to," Ginger admitted. "It reminds me of growing up in Boston."

"I do see the novelty," Basil said. "But it'll never replace the English's thirst for a good cup of tea."

"I hope not," Ginger said with a smile.

After they had appeased their hunger, their conversation turned back to the case.

"You're a good judge of character, Ginger," Basil said. "What do you make of Mr. Ryerson?"

"I do think he's sincere. It's frightfully odd, though, that Reginald Peck would be so admired in one setting and quite reviled in another."

"Blood is thicker than water," Basil said, "and hatred can run as deeply as love. In particular, the parental relationship can be tricky."

Ginger noted the twitch at the corner of Basil's mouth and thought it not the best moment to remind him that his parents were coming for dinner that evening.

"Which brings us back to Matthew Peck," Ginger said. "He's quickly becoming our prime suspect."

"Indeed. Mr. Ryerson, though tactful, didn't express any confidence in him. Matthew Peck himself admitted to an ongoing row over money. His mental capacities since the war are in question."

"He had motive and opportunity," Ginger said. "I only wish we knew exactly what the poison was. It would dearly help to point us to means."

"I couldn't agree more," Basil said. "Though, it's too soon to rule out everyone else."

"Mr. and Mrs. Northcott are an interesting pair," Ginger said. "I fail to see any mutual admiration, and I quite believe Matthew Peck's assertion that Mrs. Northcott married out of spite."

"But how does their unhappy alliance relate to our murder? What did either of them have to gain, besides a possible eviction from the house, should Mrs. Peck inherit it?"

"Mrs. Peck is in a rather unenviable position," Ginger said. "At least with Mr. Peck alive, she had someone to appeal to when one of his children rose up against her. It's three against one now."

Basil wiped his mouth with a napkin and drank the last of his soda drink, this time without the look of distaste crossing his face. Ginger did believe that Basil was warming up to the beverage.

"What's your next move?" Ginger asked.

"It's only prudent I speak to the rest of the staff at the Peck house. There's yet a possibility for another motive to be uncovered."

Ginger checked her wristwatch. "I think I should catch up with Felicia at the office. Would you mind dropping me off at my motorcar?"

"Not at all." Basil held Ginger's chair as she rose and then he put on his trilby. "I can bring you up to date on the interviews later, assuming I learn anything new."

WHEN GINGER RETURNED to Lady Gold Investigations, she found the main door unlocked and the office area empty. Felicia's red cloche hat and lacy summer gloves had been discarded on the desk.

"Felicia?"

"Darkroom. Don't come in!"

The darkroom, which had once been a cleaning cupboard, was only large enough for one person, and Ginger would have to content herself with waiting until the images had been processed through the developing chemicals and were pinned on the line inside to dry.

Ginger had planned to drop into Feathers & Flair, but time ticked away, and she wanted to get home at a decent hour to check up on Scout. She also wanted enough time to prepare for Basil's parents. It wasn't every day that one met one's in-laws for the first time, and Ginger wanted to make a perfect first impression.

A telephone call to Feathers & Flair reassured Ginger all was well on that front. She spent her time preparing a pot of tea and brought the tray to the coffee table that sat between the two chairs in front of her desk.

Felicia joined her looking rather perplexed. "I'm afraid I'm not as good at taking photographs as you, Ginger. I think I need a little practice in the darkroom as well."

"Did none of them turn out?" Ginger strolled into the darkroom to examine Felicia's work. Perhaps she should've done the assignment herself, but she would've missed out on the interviews with Basil, and those had turned out to be quite enlightening.

"Oh, well, enough to tell that our client's sister did do as she said, it's just that the images are a little blurry. Perhaps I should follow her again tomorrow and get better photographs. He will hardly be impressed with our abilities if I hand him these, and I'd hate to be responsible for ruining your reputation as an exemplary investigator."

Ginger studied the hanging images and held in the frown she felt pulling at her lips. She had to agree. They certainly couldn't hand over these as proof of their job well done.

"I suppose we'd better take another run at it." Ginger sighed. She hated giving up time from the Peck mystery to ease the nerves of an insecure brother.

"I'll do it," Felicia said.

"I don't know—"

"I know what I did wrong. I was just too excited. I have to remain calm, and I shall. I can do this, Ginger. I don't want you to feel like you can't trust me."

"I do trust you. It's not a matter of trust."

"If I mess up again, I promise never to ask for another case."

"Very well, Felicia," Ginger said. She could never say no to Felicia's spirit and enthusiasm. "But let's go over the process of successful camera operation again, shall we?"

CHAPTER THIRTEEN

When Basil returned to the Pecks, he was hardly welcomed with open arms. It seemed to Basil that Murphy's scowl had grown more profound, even in the short time Basil had been away.

Constable Braxton had remained on site and greeted him. "Chief Inspector."

"Constable. How goes the battle?"

"Just fine, sir, though my presence is barely tolerated. Mrs. Johnson was kind enough to provide a sandwich, though she made it clear it was due to her civic duty and not for love of the police."

"Righto," Basil said. "I'd like to continue the interviews with the staff." His gaze moved to the butler, who stood far enough away to be discreet yet close enough to be immediately available if called upon.

Basil wouldn't doubt he was playing loyal guard for the family as well. "Mr. Murphy," he said, raising his voice, "Would you mind if we had a quick word."

"Certainly, sir."

Murphy led them to the breakfast room where the other staff interviews had been held. The room wasn't too fancy for the below stairs' types, yet perfectly acceptable for members of the police.

Murphy nearly refused to sit, so accustomed was he to standing. His eyes pinched with suspicion, and his lips tightened. Basil doubted the butler would give much information. Like most well-trained butlers, his loyalty to his master and household would be fierce, and it went against a butler's strong principles to speak openly about anything that happened behind closed doors.

"Mr. Murphy, in your role as butler, did Mr. Peck ever confide in you?"

"No, sir. That privilege would land on Mr. Barlow."

"Mr. Peck's valet?"

"Yes, sir."

"I understand you assisted Mr. Peck in the conservatory?" Basil asked. Murphy had opportunity and means, but as yet, Basil couldn't pinpoint a motive.

"Yes, sir. I just followed Mr. Peck's instructions. He was the one with green fingers. I'm sorry for what might happen to all his flowers and plants now that he's gone."

"Did Mr. Peck have any enemies that you are aware of?"

"No, sir."

The butler was proving to be as uncooperative as Basil had feared.

"Mr. Murphy, had you noticed a decline in Mr. Peck's health recently? More rapid than in the past?"

Murphy conceded. "Well, he had been declining steadily over the last few months, Chief Inspector. However, I suppose if a person were paying attention to such things, he did seem to complain more regularly about a stomach ailment."

"How would you describe your relationship with Mr. Peck?"

"He was a good employer. He knew he was going and had already written a reference for me. He even said I should leave him early should a good position come up, but I'd never have done that, sir."

"Thank you, Mr. Murphy. That will be all for now. Perhaps you could arrange for Mr. Barlow to come and see me."

Murphy bowed and left the room.

"What do you think, sir?" Braxton said.

"I think it's easier to peel an onion than get the truth from these people."

"You think one of them did it, then?"

"It's the most probable conclusion."

Mr. Barlow was a stout man with a ring of grey hair around a bald head, and he had a friendly face—the kind that appears to be in a perpetual smile, even when one is in mourning.

"Mr. Barlow," Basil said, "I know this is a difficult time, but I'm afraid I must ask you a few questions."

"Of course. Anything that might help, sir."

"How long have you been Mr. Peck's valet?"

"Since he was a young man, sir. Nearly half a century. I'm soon to retire, you see."

Basil whistled. "That's a long time in service to one person."

"Indeed," Barlow said simply.

"I take it that Mr. Peck was an easy fellow to work for, then?"

"Most of the time, sir. He was a bit prickly near the end if you know what I mean, but that comes with dealing with a lot of pain, I suspect. He was never unkind to me."

"You see, Mr. Barlow," Basil said, leaning in, "this is what I don't understand. Everyone who worked for him thinks he was the grandest fellow, but that's not what I'm gathering from the members of his family. Can you explain the contradiction?"

Mr. Barlow shifted, inhaled, and then exhaled deeply. "I cannot."

"Mr. Barlow, might I remind you that this is a murder investigation."

"Yes, yes, of course. I just can't believe it."

"Did Mr. Peck confide in you?" Basil asked. "Did he mention anything or anyone that he was cross with or who had made him defensive in any way?"

"Mr. Peck and I spoke only of noncontroversial matters, never of his business, and certainly not about his family."

"I see. So, you can think of no one who would wish to see him dead?"

"No, sir."

Basil sighed. Onions, indeed.

Mrs. Peck's lady's maid, Miss Clarice Lawson, a woman nearer to Mrs. Peck's age in her forties, proved to be even less forthcoming than Barlow had been. She professed admiration for her lady, and had nothing untoward to report amongst the members of the household. She had nothing to gain by Mr. Peck's death and was rarely in the same room as him.

The final person from below stairs was the housekeeper, Mrs. McCullagh. Basil had meant to interview her much earlier on, but the day had gone its own way.

Mrs. McCullagh entered the breakfast room with a stern expression on her round face. "I'm not sure what I can tell you that you haven't already learned from your interviews with everyone else."

"How long have you been managing the staff in the Peck house?" Basil asked.

"Eleven years."

"So, before Mrs. Virginia Peck was a resident?"

Mrs. McCullagh pursed her lips, and Basil got the impression that Mrs. McCullagh wasn't pleased with Mr. Peck's choice of wife.

"Things were run much differently under the first Mrs. Peck," she said.

Basil prompted, "How so?"

"The first Mrs. Peck was more, shall we say, organised and content. She didn't change her mind about what it was she thought she wanted. She trusted me with my duties. Mrs. Virginia Peck constantly looks over my shoulder, changing the days off of various staff, instructing me on how to run things when I'm quite competent myself. I'm still here, aren't I? With all the special events she hosts, she'd fall on her face if it weren't for me."

Finally, a staff member willing to talk, Basil thought. "Is Mrs. Virginia Peck not well liked by the staff?"

"Let's just say we try to stay out of her way. Fault

will always be found by someone who demands perfection but inserts herself in such a way as to prevent it."

"Does she know you feel this way about her?" Basil asked.

Mrs. McCullagh blanched. "I certainly wouldn't say it to her face. It's a hard job here, but I could do worse. I'm speaking freely because you are the police, and this is *murder*."

"Do you think Mrs. Peck killed her husband?" Basil asked.

"I can't think why she would. It wasn't like she and Mr. Peck lived in each other's pockets. Mrs. Peck has everything she wants at her beck and call."

Basil wondered about the contents of Mr. Peck's will and if Mrs. Peck's life would change much now that her husband was dead.

"Can you think of anyone else who might've wanted an early demise for Mr. Peck?" Basil asked.

"I cannot," Mrs. McCullagh said. "It's well known that the children are rotten, but I can't picture any of them doing something so evil."

CHAPTER FOURTEEN

Ginger and Felicia were pulled out of their photography studies by the chimes of the bell over the door.

"Mrs. Northcott?" Ginger said, barely holding in her surprise. The grieving daughter wore a black lace dropped-waist frock with silk stockings and black pumps. A black cloche hat's veil covered half the lady's face.

"Hello, Mrs. Reed." Deirdre Northcott's gaze darted to Felicia with a look of dismay.

Ginger hurried to make an introduction. "Mrs. Northcott, this is my assistant, Miss Gold. Please have a seat."

"Miss Gold?" Mrs. Northcott snorted as she took the proffered chair. "A family affair?"

"Well, yes, I suppose it is," Ginger said.

Mrs. Northcott's brow inched up. "And you trust one another? From my experience, that's a rare situation indeed. Especially amongst families."

Ginger concurred. "It appears we are blessed in that matter." Ginger sat in the leather chair behind the desk whilst Felicia sat unobtrusively alongside a small table with a notepad and fountain pen at the ready.

"So, Mrs. Northcott," Ginger said amiably. "How can we help you today?"

"I'm not sure if you can help me. I fear I'm beyond that now, but I may be able to help you."

Ginger inclined her head. "Oh?"

"It's about Mr. Wilding."

"Mrs. Peck's family friend?"

"Yes. There's something about him I don't trust."

"Can you be more specific?"

"It's the way he makes himself at home and examines the contents of the house like he's making a mental inventory. And he doesn't seem to work or have anything to do to occupy his time, other than have tea with Virginia. It seems awfully uncouth to hang around when one has suffered the loss of a family member."

Ginger thought Mrs. Northcott had a valid point. "Mrs. Northcott, why are you here?"

"I want you to dig into Mr. Wilding's past, Mrs.

Reed. There's something amiss there, I just know it. I'm excellent at sensing these kinds of things."

"When did Mr. Wilding begin his stay at your house?" Ginger asked.

"Three weeks ago. He's begun to smell like rotten fish, as the saying goes. When I asked Papa about him, he only shrugged and suggested I let Virginia have her fun whilst she still could."

Whilst she still could? How very cryptic, Ginger thought.

"What kind of fun? Did your father suspect an affair between Mrs. Peck and Mr. Wilding?"

"I wouldn't be surprised. Virginia sees herself as quite a fox and not beyond snaring a younger man."

Ginger pushed a wayward lock of her red hair behind her ears. "But to do so underneath your father's nose does seem rather brash."

"I can't say if there's merit to Papa's suspicions, only that Virginia and Mr. Wilding are particularly chummy. I can't say I've actually seen with my own eyes anything untoward. That doesn't mean anything, of course."

"Has Mrs. Peck spoken of Mr. Wilding in the past? Has he visited before?"

"No. This is the first any of us had ever heard of Mr. Wilding, which is surprising since Virginia claims to have known Mr. Wilding since he was a baby."

"How old is Mr. Wilding?" This came from Felicia. Mrs. Northcott cast a glance her way, then spoke to Ginger. "He's twenty-four."

"Do you have reason to suspect that Mr. Wilding might've had something to do with your father's death?" Ginger asked.

"He's the only stranger in the house. As much as my husband and brother caused me consternation, and to my father when he was alive, God bless his soul, they're not killers." Deirdre Northcott took a moment to pat the end of her nose with her handkerchief. "I'll pay you, of course."

Ginger revealed her fees.

"That is satisfactory," Mrs. Northcott said as she got to her feet. "If you need to reach me, please leave a message with Murphy saying that my hat has arrived. I'll contact you. Please do not come to the house."

Ginger and Felicia watched as Mrs. Northcott left, and the sound of the door chime followed her out.

"*My hat has arrived,*" Felicia said. "I like that. So covert sounding."

Ginger only hummed. At least Mrs. Northcott hadn't forbidden her to tell anyone she'd engaged Lady Gold Investigations, which meant she could share whatever she discovered with Basil.

"Where do we start?" Felicia said with eagerness.

Her sister-in-law seemed to be enjoying participating in the investigation.

"I thought I employed you to man the telephone," Ginger said. "Don't you have a book to write?"

"Oh, bother. This is so much more fun! And I've already told you, I have a creative blockage."

"Very well," Ginger said. "Let's go see what we can find out about Mr. Wilding."

CHAPTER FIFTEEN

*I*t seemed judicious to Basil to interview the neighbours. Since the Peck residence was the house on the corner, the walls were shared with only one neighbour, the elderly Lord and Lady Clifford.

A stout but straight-backed butler answered the door, and Basil introduced himself and Constable Braxton. "We're here in relation to the death next door," Basil said. "We hate to inconvenience Lord and Lady Clifford, but it is a matter of police business."

The butler acknowledged Basil's request but kept his expression bland, though his small eyes did flash momentarily with annoyance.

The butler ushered Basil and Braxton into the drawing room where Lord and Lady Clifford already sat. Basil and his constable took a seat opposite their hosts, and Basil had to admire the efficiency of some households.

"Such dreadful news," Lady Clifford said. Though he'd seen the genteel lady in a photo in the society pages, and most recently in the dim light of the Pecks' ballroom, up close and in the light of day, Basil was bemused by the number of deep lines that mapped her face. He now thought her to be several years older than he had the evening before.

Lady Clifford, thankfully, was unaware of Basil's inner musings. She continued, "To think that something so criminal could happen here on Eaton Square."

"Crime doesn't have the social barriers one would wish for," Basil said.

Lady Clifford pursed her lips but remained silent.

"I'm not sure we can be of much help to you, Chief Inspector," Lord Clifford said. He seemed to be aging better than his wife, though he might have been younger than her by some years. Basil couldn't be sure.

"You and Lady Clifford were in attendance at the Pecks' gala last night," Basil stated.

Lady Clifford sniffed. "It's hard for one to say no to an invitation when one lives next door."

"You didn't get on?" Basil asked.

"Mrs. Peck is quite a young thing," Lady Clifford said. "The young have strange ways, as you might agree, Constable Braxton?"

Basil held in a grin as he nodded to Braxton to respond.

"I've heard society has most definitely changed since the turn of the century," Braxton said.

A young maid scurried in with a tea trolley, poured the tea, and offered biscuits.

"Have you noticed anything unusual happening next door lately?" Basil asked once they'd settled in.

"We've failed to find anything *usual*," Lady Clifford said. "It's nonstop coming and going, and those Peck individuals haven't a modicum of propriety. I've seen them yelling at each other on the pavement!"

In Basil's line of work, he'd encountered many sorts of families, and he had to agree with Lady Clifford; this one seemed exceptionally unorthodox.

"Lord Clifford," Basil began, "did you and Mr. Peck ever meet socially over the years? Over drinks, perhaps, or a game of cards?"

"It's been several years since his health problems became apparent. He was once a vibrant, capable man, though, from what I can deduce, his business instincts were as good as ever. But since he'd become an invalid, I can't say I'd seen him about much at all. Only when good manners required that we attend one of Mrs. Peck's social events."

"How often does she host such an event?" Braxton asked.

"Every couple of months, I'd say," Lady Clifford said.

Lord Clifford sat upright. "Not to be disrespectful to Mr. Peck's memory, but I'll be grateful to have a break from Mrs. Peck's incessant need to entertain."

Lady Clifford scoffed. "Her need is not to entertain; her need is to be the centrepiece of her perfect home."

Sometimes, Basil thought, it was best to just get to the point. He asked, "Can you think of anyone who'd have reason to kill Mr. Peck?"

Lord and Lady Clifford exchanged a look. Lady Clifford shook her head slowly. Lord Clifford worked his lips in decision. Basil willed him to speak forth. He was rewarded.

"I know the spotlight will be on his spoiled offspring, but I saw Mr. Peck and his solicitor exchanging heated words last night. I can't be certain, but I thought I heard one of them say they were tempted to do something rash if a certain something wasn't done."

Basil's heart skipped a beat as it always did when a potential lead presented itself. "Do you recall what that 'something' was?"

Lord Clifford blew rapidly through dry lips. "I'm afraid I didn't catch the details. The musicians were frightfully loud."

Basil and Braxton excused themselves and were shown out by the Cliffords' butler.

"They seem a harmless pair," Braxton said. "Though they didn't have a lot of respect for Mrs. Peck."

"Nor Mr. Peck," Basil said. "I do wonder what he and Winthrop were on about."

AFTER MOVING INTO HARTIGAN HOUSE, it had taken Basil a few weeks to become comfortable there. Unlike his townhouse in Mayfair where he lived a peaceful and mostly solitary life, Hartigan House was often a bustle of activity. Clement would greet Basil in the back garden after he parked his Austin. Mrs. Beasley stayed out of view, but her voice carried as she barked orders to one or another of the maids. Pippins, like an apparition, appeared out of nowhere to take Basil's hat and gloves, and coat when the weather required.

Ambrosia had an aura about her that extended like the rings of Saturn, her aura filling whatever room she was in, and Felicia had inherited the same abilities, albeit, hers was of the more delightful sort. All the Gold ladies had a larger-than-life personality, including his own wife—no longer technically a Gold lady.

Ginger was always a welcome presence, and unlike the others, Basil felt rejuvenated in her company. It was her intellect as much as her charm that drew him.

As often as not, one of the maids, Lizzie usually, cleaned the staircase, either by polishing the rails or vacuuming the carpet. He passed her with a nod of his head, and she offered a slight curtsy.

It was a relief to finally get to one's private bedroom.

Ginger had done a nice job of making room for him. Another wardrobe had been brought in, and Basil stepped out of his suit, hung the pinstripe linen trousers inside his wardrobe, and placed the soiled garments into the appropriate basket. Once he'd changed into casual trousers and shirt, he settled into one of the white and gold striped chairs that flanked a circular table under the windows. A folded evening paper waited there as per Basil's request, along with a neat whisky. He flipped the newspaper open.

He was happy with the headlines—neither a murder nor a scandal—and read purely for the routine. He gratefully allowed his mind an opportunity to rest. In his line of work, one's job could eclipse one's life if one wasn't careful.

Someone had written a short interest piece on Ginger's charity, The Child Wellness Project, a meal service she and the Reverend Oliver Hill of St.

George's Anglican Church had started. Basil was pleased with the positive slant the journalist had taken on how the project helped to keep street children from the brink of starvation, and also from the crime hunger seemed to breed.

He smiled to himself, thinking that he'd have to remember to show Ginger the story. Then he thought about Scout Elliot, a former street child who had benefitted from the meals. A charmer to be sure, and most certainly having the skills to survive on the streets. Though with his impish grin and childlike posture, Basil understood why Ginger had been drawn to the lad.

And now, Basil was to become the boy's father.

He sipped his drink.

It wasn't that he never wanted to be a father. He had hoped to conceive with his first wife and might have if she hadn't deceived him with her use of preventive measures without his knowledge. She hadn't been the motherly type, nor the faithful sort, as it turned out.

Ginger was entirely different. Basil knew that Ginger had desperately wanted children with her late husband, Daniel, but mother nature had had different plans. Ginger had warned Basil before they'd wed that she might physically be responsible for her childlessness, a possibility that never concerned him. Basil was over ten years Ginger's senior and could just as easily give up on the idea of fatherhood, but Ginger was still a young woman.

Adoption was always an option, he supposed. Basil had thought they'd begin with an infant, not a child nearing puberty. But if this was what Ginger wanted, and she'd made it clear that she did, then Basil wouldn't get in the way of it happening. He'd vowed to make Ginger happy, and therefore, he'd put his best effort into providing for Scout and giving him guidance in this world.

A deep inhale and Basil was ready to face what he'd mentally come to call, with endearment, the Hartigan Hordes.

Before he could make a move, Pippins interrupted his thoughts. Basil raised a brow in question as Pippins always respected Basil's privacy and didn't interfere with his times of solitude without a good reason.

"Yes, Pippins?"

"I'm sorry to intrude, sir, but your parents have arrived."

CHAPTER SIXTEEN

hat Ginger wanted was a police check on Cyril Wilding so when she returned to Hartigan House and saw Basil standing in the back garden, it was the first thing she mentioned after greeting him with a kiss.

"Mrs. Deirdre Northcott came to the office with deep concerns about Mrs. Peck's house guest, and—"

"Ginger?" Basil tried to interrupt.

"I've promised to look into his history for her, to make sure nothing is amiss. I would so appreciate it if you could look into his background. You've probably done so already, haven't you? As part of your murder enquiries."

"Ginger?"

Ginger's mind skipped off the track of the case long

enough to see the flash of worry behind Basil's eyes. He stopped her outside the back door.

"Basil? Is something wrong?"

Her mind immediately went to Scout. The lad was usually in the back garden to greet her. "Has something happened to Scout?"

Basil's hand rested on her shoulder. "No, love. He's fine. He's around here somewhere."

Ginger placed a hand on her chest and willed her pulse to slow. "What is it then?"

"We've got visitors."

"Oh mercy. Your parents are here already?"

"They thought they'd drop in for an aperitif."

Ginger glanced down at the suit ensemble she'd left the house in that morning. She felt wilted and desperate for a bath and certainly didn't want to meet the Honourable Henry and Mrs. Anna Reed in the condition she looked and felt in at that moment.

"Where are they now?" she asked.

"In the drawing room."

"Please distract them whilst I hurry upstairs to change. I do want to make a good first impression."

"You're absolutely lovely just as you are."

"Basil."

"Fine, but please don't make me spend too much time alone with them."

"Why? I thought you got on with your parents?"

"Oh, I do. Very well. So long as they are residing in another country."

Boss bounded towards the sound of Ginger's voice. "Hello, Bossy," she said as she bent to scoop him up. "I need you to help me choose an evening gown."

Basil disappeared behind the drawing room doors as Ginger headed up the staircase. Lizzie met her in the corridor.

"I've selected a couple of gowns for you, madam, and they're lying out on the bed."

"Thank you, Lizzie, you are a lifesaver."

Lizzie followed Ginger into her room. "I thought you'd like a change before meeting Mr. and Mrs. Reed."

"You thought right!"

Changing one's wardrobe was always faster when one had a lady's maid to assist. Soon, Ginger stepped out of her cotton suit and into a cream and lavender satin gown. With lavender straps, the creamy bodice sparkled with sequins. A lovely lavender tiered fringe hung in angling layers from her waist on the right to the opposite hip. A string of pearls finished the look.

At the dressing table, Lizzie brushed Ginger's hair and added two brass fan-shaped art deco pins. Ginger preferred to do her own makeup. Her eyebrows, arched widely, needed a little touching up. She filled them in with smoky eye shadow then added a thick layer of mascara to her lashes. Two spots of rouge highlighted her cheeks, and she painted her lips to look like a tight bow.

"How do I look?"

"Lovely, madam," Lizzie answered with a hint of awe and envy. "As always."

"What do you think, Boss? Shall I impress the in-laws?"

Boss barked once before relaxing into his casual doggy smile.

Ginger didn't know a lot about Basil's parents except that they were wealthy and eclectic, loved to spend time on their yacht, and travelled to places like South Africa and India. They could be passionate about living adventurously. They'd once adopted an African child who not long afterwards had been tragically murdered. The case was still unsolved, and Basil had confided in her once that the ordeal was one of the things that had sparked his interest in policing.

Ginger loved adventurous and eccentric people, and she was sure that she would adore her new family. But would they feel the same way about her?

Ginger took a moment outside the drawing room to gather herself. She didn't know why she felt so nervous, as she had no reason to be. This was her home, and it was impressive. She was British, had married into the peerage, and had her own wealth. She was a good match for their son.

Ginger grabbed both handles of the French doors to the drawing room and opened them wide as she stepped inside. Newly decorated, the room now had fewer furnishings and paintings than the previous Edwardian décor, with lighter curtains in a pale rose shade, and walls painted and papered in tones of mint-green and ivory. The eye was immediately drawn to a large brick fireplace, and off to the side, a baby grand piano.

The Reed family sat on the new furniture, a green velvet settee with matching pincushion armchairs, all trimmed ornately with dark wood. Basil's father stood and offered his hand. Ginger could see where Basil's good looks came from. His father had the same build and warm hazel eyes. His mother carried her age well, with shiny dark hair shingled in perfect finger waves, and skin that was freckled slightly from her time in sunny climates.

"You must be Georgia," Mrs. Reed declared. She wore a delicate French-style evening gown, a Madeleine Violet if Ginger wasn't mistaken. Bold red layers of chemise were trimmed in gold, with an attached scarf on the right shoulder. "Or, Ginger," Mrs. Reed corrected, "Basil tells us."

"You may call me whatever you like," Ginger said

with a smile. She shook her in-laws' hands, and then the four were seated.

Pippins brought her a sherry. "Thank you, Pippins," she said, refraining from her more familiar address of "Pips".

"You're welcome, madam."

Once Ginger had settled in one of the armchairs, Mrs. Reed said, "This is a delightful little house."

Ginger chose to ignore the slight at the size, knowing that the Reeds main home was a manor. "Thank you, Mrs. Reed. It's home."

The Reeds regaled Ginger and Basil with stories of their travels, and Ginger thought they were getting along quite swimmingly. Pippins returned and announced that dinner was served.

"Oh, splendid," Mrs. Reed said. "We've been doing all the talking and can catch up on your adventures while we eat."

Mrs. Beasley had rounded up all the staff to assist with the important meal, including a new young scullery maid, Daphne, who replaced Scout's efforts.

A large oval table was centred in the rectangular dining room and was set with Ginger's best china. Overhead, a lovely electric chandelier cast warm slivers of light.

As the hosts, Basil and Ginger each took an end of

the table with Ambrosia and Felicia on one side and Mr. and Mrs. Reed on the other.

The evening started with a bowl of onion soup, which was followed by Sole Colbert seasoned and fried to perfection. Pippins had produced a bottle of Château Margaux from Ginger's collection as an accompaniment. Ginger had spent time selecting the menu for this evening and knew the main course of roast lamb with mint sauce and seasoned carrots was to follow.

"We regret missing your nuptials," Mr. Reed said after a bite, "but we were in Cape Town, and even if we'd left the day after we received Basil's telegram, we wouldn't have made it on time."

Ginger noted the hint of disapproval, but she had to admit that she and Basil had wed rather quickly—perhaps six months too soon for propriety—after the death of his first wife, Emelia.

"I, for one, don't see the attraction," Ambrosia said. Ginger shot her a startled look.

"I mean," the dowager clarified, "in Africa. It's hot and dirty, from what I can tell. I prefer to keep my feet in England."

"We enjoy mingling with other cultures," Mrs. Reed said.

Ginger didn't miss the slight edge in her voice.

"It's the diamonds, Grandmama," Felicia said. "If it

weren't for that, no English blood would bother."

"I beg to differ, Miss Gold," Mr. Reed said.

Ginger was relieved to see his eyes betrayed amusement. "The spices, and fauna. The scent in the air is exotic."

"The beaches are delightful to bathe on," Mrs. Reed added.

"It's true, we are short on hot weather to enjoy lounging on the sand," Ginger said, "though I've heard Brighton is quite popular in the summer." She smiled at Basil. "We should go there sometime."

Basil smiled in return. "Certainly."

The meal ended with a sponge Napoleon dessert.

"Your cook has outdone herself," Mrs. Reed said generously.

Ginger agreed. "Mrs. Beasley is a wonder. She'll be delighted that you enjoyed her efforts."

Afterwards, Basil and his father remained in the dining room for a glass of port, and the ladies reclined in the sitting room.

"You don't mind if I run off, do you?" Felicia said before they'd even got seated. "I've promised Alison I'd meet up with her tonight."

"You know how I feel about you gallivanting after dark," Ambrosia said.

"It's hardly dark, Grandmama. It's summertime.

And stepping out with one's good friend is hardly galli-vanting."

Felicia disappeared, and when Ambrosia claimed exhaustion to follow her soon afterwards, Ginger suddenly found herself alone with her mother-in-law.

"Oh good," Mrs. Reed said as if the Gold ladies had left them at her request. "I hoped to have some time alone to really chat."

Ginger sipped her sherry and crossed her legs. "I suppose you would have questions for me. How much has Basil told you about how we met?"

"He wrote us a lengthy letter, quite boyish in his exclamations about your virtues. A rather nice change from the morose tomes about Emelia."

Basil's marriage to his late wife, Emelia, had been less than blissful.

"I'm quite relieved in the end that they never produced a child together."

Ginger pushed a lock of red hair behind her ear and shifted in her chair. Had Basil hinted to his parents that childlessness, at least the traditional way, would also be the case for them? "Yes, well, things of this nature can't always be counted on."

"To be honest, I thought you would be younger," Mrs. Reed said. "I never asked outright, of course, but by the way Basil described you."

Ginger held her countenance, not giving away the

offence she felt at that moment. Her wartime training often came in handy. Thirty-one wasn't that terribly old.

"I like to think of myself as young at heart," Ginger said.

CHAPTER SEVENTEEN

The atmosphere at the Peck house the next day was sombre. At its worst, there was an underlying tremor, as if an earthquake were about to shake the foundations at any moment. Apart from Ginger—who wore a green long-sleeved silk blouse with a high, wide collar and embellished with a decorative row of off-centred buttons, along with a coordinated tri-coloured pleated skirt—everyone was wearing black.

All the family members were present in the drawing room along with Mr. Wilding, a fact Ginger found curious. She wasn't the only one.

"What's he doing here?" Matthew Peck demanded.

Virginia Peck sat upright with her chin jutted,

"He's here at my request. Moral support, you could say."

Ginger didn't blame the young matriarch. The stepchildren eyed her narrowly, beaks sharpened.

As for Ginger's presence, the family seemed to have grown used to her accompanying Basil, and aside from a raised eyebrow or disinterested scowl, they ignored her.

A table had been set up as a makeshift desk, and Mr. Winthrop sat behind it, a file sitting importantly in front of him. A briefcase was propped up against the table leg.

"Can we just get this circus over with," Alastair Northcott said. "We all know everything's going to Matthew."

A gasp escaped Mrs. Peck's lips. "He wouldn't leave me destitute, Mr. Winthrop," she said weakly. "Would he?"

Mr. Winthrop cleared his throat. "Let's get started, shall we?"

Ginger and Basil had orchestrated their seating, Basil on one side and Ginger on the other, both with a view of the family members' faces.

Alastair Northcott, languid in his red and gold *kurta*, sat next to his wife, Deirdre, who'd cast a glance at Ginger and then a questioning brow toward Mr. Wilding. The object of Mrs. Northcott's consternation was the only person left standing. He leaned against the back of the pincushion-backed chair occupied by Virginia Peck.

Matthew cradled his weak arm as his knees jumped as if he were playing an invisible drum kit. His agitation was palpable. Ginger wondered what caused such nervousness in the young man, especially if he was favoured to inherit. Then again, such tension seemed his normal constitution.

Mr. Winthrop licked his lips. "This is the last will and testament of Mr. Reginald Peck, signed on the third of March 1925."

Three months ago, Ginger mused. If someone had wanted the will changed recently, he or she hadn't succeeded.

Mr. Winthrop's gaze flickered upwards briefly before settling back on the text in front of him. His hands shook slightly as he held the document.

"Come on, man," Mr. Northcott said. "Put us out of our misery."

"I, Reginald Peck Esquire, being of sound mind, do bequeath, upon my death, the following:

"To my son, Matthew, I bequeath forty-nine percent of my business holdings."

Matthew's eyes twitched. He was two percent short of a majority, which failed to give him controlling shares, Ginger thought. Surely, the other fifty-one would be divided, though, leaving him the primary stakeholder.

Mr. Winthrop continued, "To my darling wife, Virginia Peck, I give forty percent of the shares, to be distributed as a monthly dividend."

There was a gasp of unease as comprehension descended. This condition prevented Mrs. Peck from taking hold of her share of the fortune at once, and Ginger noticed the lady worked tense lips in her silence.

Mr. Winthrop looked over his spectacles to add a further blow. "There's a caveat that should Mrs. Peck pass away or remarry, her portion is to be given to Deirdre Northcott."

Virginia Peck breathed heavily through her nose. Should she remain single for the rest of her life, she would be well taken care of.

A two-edged sword for one still in her prime, Ginger thought.

"Is that all?" she finally said. "What about this house? Can I still live here, or is it to be sold and divided too?"

"Mr. Peck did make provisions for the house," Mr. Winthrop said. "In fact, you are to own fifty percent of the deed, Mrs. Peck."

The tightness in Virginia's features relaxed margin- ally, but her late husband's favour would show its limitations once again.

"You shall own half of the deed," the solicitor said, "as long as the conservatory and the plants therein are taken care of in the manner they have been accustomed to."

Mrs. Peck seemed unable to erase the look of embarrassment that crossed her face. "Of course, I'll care for his blasted flowers." She lowered her voice when she added, "I swear he loved those plants more than me." Her accusation earned her scathing looks from her stepchildren.

"What about me?" Deirdre Northcott asked. Ginger also wondered if Mr. Peck had gone through with his threat of cutting her out.

Mr. Winthrop continued his recitation. "To my daughter, Deirdre Northcott, I grant an eleven percent interest in Peck Properties." Mr. Winthrop stared at Mrs. Northcott and explained. "Despite your disagreements, your father didn't want to leave you with nothing."

"*She* gets forty percent," Alastair Northcott said haughtily, pointing a finger at Virginia Peck, "and his own daughter gets a measly eleven?"

"You expected nothing," Matthew quipped.

Mr. Northcott growled.

Very unseemly for someone who professed to live

life under a state of meditative calmness, Ginger thought.

"I'm afraid, it's even less for you, Mr. Northcott," Mr. Winthrop added. "Mrs. Northcott's shares are to be in her name only; these and," he cast a glance at Virginia Peck, "any others she may acquire over time."

"You mean *my* shares," Mrs. Peck said tersely. "I suppose I'll have to watch my back."

Deirdre scoffed. "I'm not a killer, Virginia."

"Well, someone is." This came from Cyril Wilding, most unwisely.

"Maybe it was you, Mr. Wilding," Mrs. Northcott said. "Daddy was doing just fine before you came to visit. Isn't it about time you went back to wherever you came from?"

Virginia jumped to her feet. "He'll stay for as long as I desire. I'm still mistress of this house."

Matthew Peck jumped from his chair and stabbed Mr. Wilding in the chest with his finger. "And I'm the master!"

Cyril Wilding responded by thrusting Matthew Peck with a two-handed shove, which caused the gentleman to land ungracefully on the soft cushions of the settee. He immediately sprang to his feet, his anger causing his cheeks to burst with colour. "How dare you!"

Basil stepped between the men before pandemonium broke out, and held out his arms to create an imagined force that kept the outraged men apart. Speaking loudly, and with admirable authority, he said, "Stay calm, everyone. Nothing is to be gained by losing one's head."

CHAPTER EIGHTEEN

*C*onstable Braxton was manning the main desk when Ginger and Basil arrived at Scotland Yard. It was easy for Ginger to understand why Felicia would be soft on him and she wondered if he already had a sweetheart.

"Busy day, Constable Braxton?" she asked lightly. Basil had disappeared into his office, leaving Ginger in the lobby free to chat.

"Yes, madam. Crime never slows in a city like London."

"I suppose not, but Superintendent Morris can't work you all the time." Though, knowing what she did of the narrow-minded and often belligerent superintendent, it wouldn't have come as a surprise to Ginger if he had his underlings working their legs off.

"Nine- to twelve-hour shifts, madam, six days a week."

"That is quite a lot."

"I don't mind it," the constable said. "It'll help me rise in the ranks if I pay my dues. Nothing like experience to train a man."

"An outstanding attitude, Constable. A sweetheart would have to be very understanding."

Constable Braxton's Adam's apple bobbed up and down. "I would imagine. I don't have a sweetheart myself, but some of the lads here find it difficult at times to juggle work and family."

Ginger smiled, keeping the relief she felt to herself. Basil returned, ending the conversation which was teetering on becoming awkward.

Basil held a folder in his hands. "Braxton had the background checks I'd asked for."

Ginger followed Basil to his office where he opened the folder and separated the papers into two piles. He pointed to the first one.

"These are all staff members. There's only anything of potential interest for two of them." He pushed two sheets of paper towards Ginger. "Josie Roth, the parlour maid, and Mrs. McCullagh."

"Mrs. McCullagh?" Ginger said with interest. "Wasn't she the housekeeper under the first Mrs. Peck?"

"Indeed."

"Why would she want to kill Mr. Peck? One would think she would rather remove the current mistress if she was going to kill anyone."

"As far as we know, she hasn't committed any crime," Basil said.

"Why is she a person of interest, then?"

"She lied about her credentials when taken on by the first Mrs. Peck, something that hasn't, as far as we know, come to light."

"She's managed to do an excellent job, despite it," Ginger said. "And Miss Roth?"

"Josie Roth had been let go from her previous place of service, for alleged theft."

"Why on earth would Virginia Peck employ her?"

"It would seem she didn't know."

Basil then directed Ginger's attention to the second pile. "Cyril Wilding. Twenty-four, educated at University College, London and recently graduated. Apart from a recent motorcar incident, he has no record with the police. According to his senior tutor, Cyril Wilding was considered rather antisocial, a fellow who preferred his own company. There is one record of him coming to fists with another student, but they each were given a warning, and there was nothing more recorded after that."

Basil pointed to the next name. "Matthew Peck,

twenty-nine. Army man, fought in the battle of the Somme. Educated at Cambridge. Worked for his father until he was unceremoniously sacked."

"Whatever for?"

"Apparently, he suffers from shell shock and other mental weaknesses as a result of his time in the war. Peck then jumped on a ship to South America and only returned a year ago."

"What did he do in South America?" Ginger asked.

"Brazil, to be specific. And likely, not much. He likes to dabble in the stock market."

"That could be how he supported himself there."

Basil continued on to Deirdre Northcott. "The daughter, twenty-five, was educated at a finishing school."

"How Victorian," Ginger quipped.

"Yes, well, Mr. Peck was old-fashioned that way, at least when Mrs. Northcott was a girl. It was well known amongst the neighbours on Eaton Square that Deirdre and Mr. Peck were at odds over her upbringing. Her mother, the first Mrs. Peck, was quite ill during her formative years and was unable to give her any support. Deirdre Nothcott's marriage to Alastair Northcott seems to have been an act of rebellion against her father."

"Perhaps Mr. Peck had a change of heart," Ginger

said. "He didn't write her out of the will as he'd threatened, and made it possible for her to come into a stronger position should Virginia Peck remarry."

"Quite," Basil said. "Which brings me to Virginia Peck, née Virginia Robinson."

"A beautiful young thing captures the eye of an older, established man?" Ginger smiled and batted her lashes with a glint of mischievousness. Except for the telltale grey at his temples, Ginger thought Basil looked younger than his age. She added, "It happens."

Basil chuckled. "Indeed. And that's what happened in Virginia Robinson's case. She's from Battersea—a middle-class family without connections. A certain skill and tenacity is required to adopt a sophisticated air to attract a man who's not only well-to-do but a member of the right class."

"True," Ginger said, feeling intrigued and gaining a modicum of respect for Virginia Peck. To look at her now, one would have thought she'd always had the advantages of privilege. "The question is, how did she manage? Someone, somewhere, must've given her aid."

"My thoughts exactly," Basil said. "But no matter Virginia Peck's resourcefulness and ingenuity, it doesn't mean she's a killer."

"She had means and opportunity."

Basil rubbed his chin. "They all had means and

opportunity. That's the problem. It's bound to come down to motive."

"Unless she felt certain that she was going to inherit well, killing her husband would be risky."

Basil ducked his chin. "Except that he was dying anyway."

"As you mentioned, this is true for all our suspects," Ginger said. "Which brings us to the final family member."

"Alastair Northcott, thirty-two." Basil referenced the report as he continued. "The unwanted, under-appreciated son-in-law who claims to be living a peaceful life through meditation and Eastern mysticism."

"I fail to see that he's having success at that," Ginger said, "though anyone could be forgiven for feeling strained during a family crisis such as this."

"Did he kill Mr. Peck?" Basil asked.

"Perhaps he was simply angry with his father-in-law, and he wanted to have the last word, so to speak." Ginger went on, "They might've had words that led to murder."

"In fact, Josie the parlour maid, mentioned such an instance in her statement. She was passing through the corridor outside Mr. Peck's room that morning when she heard heated voices."

"Did she hear what was said?"

"She says no, only that Northcott stormed out moments later. She'd ducked behind one of the many potted plants in the house and avoided being spotted."

Ginger could understand the instinct to duck out of sight. If a maid was under suspicion of spying or eavesdropping, it would be grounds for dismissal.

"I can understand an argument leading to murder in the passion of the moment," Ginger said. "But death by poisoning is most definitely premeditated."

Ginger picked up the report to peruse the added details, which included places and dates of birth. She handed it to Basil who returned it to the folder. He placed his trilby on his head and said, "I think it's time to have another talk with Mr. Northcott."

CHAPTER NINETEEN

A telephone call to the Pecks' provided the information Basil sought—the whereabouts of Alastair Northcott—which was why he and Ginger were currently parked in front of the Imperial Indian Society building, behind the Hindu temple.

The brightly decorated interior was reminiscent of traditional Indian décor that Basil had witnessed on one of the few journeys he'd shared with his parents: sky blues, blood oranges, lime greens. A mini shrine to His Majesty, Emperor of India, sat near the entrance, his official photograph in a wooden frame painted gold. The melodious sounds of sitar music reached Basil from some corner of the building.

Quiet enquiries pointed Basil and Ginger to a room where they found numerous people dressed in the pyjama-like *kurta*, or the female *sari*, sitting on mats with legs folded, hands pressed in a prayer position, and eyes closed.

Basil spotted Northcott in the back row. The forefinger and thumb of each hand touched and rested on each knee, and a low tone emanated from his lips in "*om, om, om.*"

When Basil tapped him on the shoulder, Northcott's inner peace seemed to shatter.

"Good God!"

Basil shared a look with Ginger. Hardly the expression one expected from a practitioner of Eastern enlightenment.

"Sorry to disturb you, Mr. Northcott," Basil said, keeping his voice low. "Might we have a word?"

Clearly ruffled, Alastair Northcott unfolded himself. With feet bared, he padded to the corridor then turned to Basil and Ginger and frowned. "It's Arjun, at least whilst I'm here."

Ginger attempted to mollify him. "Arjun, is there a place we could speak in private?"

Mr. Northcott nodded, his demeanour of peace once again under his command. "Of course. There is seating in the garden."

In the courtyard, a grouping of simple wooden benches was assembled near a fountain with a Hindu god as the centrepiece. Northcott dropped into the middle of one bench, arms spread across the back, legs splayed. Basil and Ginger claimed the one next to him.

"What is it that is so important that you had to interrupt my meditation?" Northcott asked.

"We have a statement from a member of the household that you and Mr. Peck had a heated argument only a day before his death."

"So?" Northcott said. "I wasn't the only one to argue with the old man. He was quite insufferable towards the end."

"What were you doing in Mr. Peck's bedroom?" Ginger asked.

Northcott snorted. "I wanted to speak to him on Deirdre's behalf."

"About his will?" Basil said.

"Yes. About the damned will. I was concerned that he'd go through with his threat and cut his daughter out of it. His own flesh and blood!"

"Not to mention, by extension, you," Basil added.

"Well, yes, I suppose so. I am her husband after all, and I quite bloody well hate having to live under another man's roof. I won't deny hoping for a bit to afford our own place. Nothing criminal about that."

"But Mr. Peck wouldn't appease your concerns?" Basil said. Alastair Northcott hadn't looked like a man who'd expected anything when the will was being read.

"No, the blighter. Made me sweat it out, he did."

"But you sounded unhappy with her portion?"

"Eleven percent? I expected nothing, true, but that amount will hardly give us ample funds. I fear we'll be living on Peck family charity until—" Northcott stopped suddenly as if he feared he'd dug a hole and stepped into it.

"Until Mrs. Peck dies?" Ginger asked.

"No. For Pete's sake, no. Until she marries, of course. And who knows if she'll do that. I wouldn't, that's for sure. Give up a fortune for love. Ha! What a laugh."

CHAPTER TWENTY

The open-for-business sign was already on display when Ginger reached the office of Lady Gold Investigations. After meeting with Alastair Northcott, she wanted to check on her businesses. Basil needed to return to Scotland Yard.

Felicia exited the darkroom with some eight-by-ten black and white photographs in her hands.

"I followed Mr. Soames' sister," she said, "and snapped more photographs. Hopefully, they're better than the last ones."

Ginger removed her hat and gloves and placed them on the sideboard. "Anything new to report?"

"Miss Soames is doing as she claimed. It's so sad to see families with such levels of distrust." Felicia smiled at Ginger. "I'm so glad we're not that way."

"As am I," Ginger replied, though it made her think

of her new mother-in-law and the friction that seethed under the surface.

"I mean, look at the Pecks," Felicia said, oblivious to Ginger's flash of familial angst. "Everyone suspecting the other." Her eyes widened as a new thought gripped her. "That's right, you were just at the reading of the will, weren't you? You must tell me how it went!"

Felicia followed Ginger into the kitchenette where Ginger went through the motions of making a pot of tea. "Oh mercy, a disaster. I don't know if this family will make it through this crisis intact."

"Pretty hard I imagine if one of you is a murderer. So, what happened?"

Ginger divulged the events of the morning, which had ended in a row between the houseguest and the son of the deceased.

"Oh, rather!" Felicia said. "This Cyril Wilding fellow is a mysterious figure."

Ginger poured the tea. "I learned from the background checks report that Constable Braxton put together," she noted the slight blossom of pink that appeared on Felicia's cheeks at the mention of the constable's name, but ignored it and continued, "that Mr. Wilding was born in a south London borough in 1901. Perhaps we can find more information at the General Register Office,"

"Shall we go now?"

"Might as well, though we'll have to take a taxicab. Basil dropped me off."

"Oh, let's take the tube!" Felicia said. "It's rather exciting. Taking a taxicab all the time is such a bore."

Ginger grinned. "Fine, but let's have our tea first."

It was a short walk to Piccadilly station, and Ginger and Felicia joined the throng that headed underground to await the tube train heading for Waterloo. Many passengers were businessmen dressed in dark suits and either trilby or bowler hats, their eyes cast downward with a newspaper in hand. The occasional gentleman read a book depending, Ginger imagined, on the length of the journey. The women were housewives running errands, or nannies out with their charges.

"Travelling on the tube feels daring, don't you think?" Felicia said, "In an adventurous sort of way."

Ginger smiled at Felicia's sense of awe, which suited her imaginative spirit. "I think these travellers are rather ordinary citizens than adventurers."

Felicia didn't relent. "You never know. One of them might be a spy on some kind of reconnaissance mission. Perhaps *we're* being followed."

Felicia's jest caused Ginger a moment of alarm. She cast a furtive glance around, reassuring herself that she'd have sensed if someone had been following them. Besides, what on earth would they be worth pursuing?

Unless the killer was having them watched?

Ginger was quite happy when, a short time later, the train pulled into Waterloo station, and they climbed the steps near Waterloo Bridge. The General Register Office was in the North Wing of Somerset House, eastward.

Inside, Ginger made enquires of the clerk. "I'm Lady Gold of Lady Gold Investigations, and this is my assistant Miss Gold. We're looking for a birth record for a client, a Mr. Cyril Wilding," she said. "He was born in Battersea in the year 1901."

"We're desperate to find him," added Felicia. "An inheritance is involved."

Ginger shot Felicia a quizzical look, but Felicia's ruse seemed to strike a chord.

"A young man's deserving of the family jewels, I suppose," the man said. "Here's what we got on Wildings from Battersea in that year. Not a lot, mind, but hopefully you'll find what you're looking for."

"Thank you, sir," Ginger said. She waited for the clerk to step away then opened the files.

"Edward and Mary Wilding," she said with interest. "Oh, look at this death certificate. The child's name was also Cyril, but the date of death is 1900."

"A child can't die before it's been born," Felicia

said. "Perhaps these are the wrong parents for our Cyril Wilding."

"Perhaps." Ginger's mind went to another couple she'd known, years ago back in Boston. "Unless—"

"Unless what?" Felicia asked.

"Unless a secret adoption took place. One child to replace the other. An adoption. Those aren't registered."

Though there were rumours that change was coming, adoption had no legal status in Britain. Because of her intentions for Scout, Ginger had been doing her research. Child adoption was an informal arrangement, and often secretive. For an unmarried woman to have a child would be not only a social disgrace but often meant financial destitution. Giving away one's child was often the only recourse.

It was a risk for the adoptive parents as well. Even if money exchanged hands, the biological mother could legally demand custody of their child at any time, despite social repercussions, and perhaps continue to make financial demands.

"Sometimes mothers in distress sell their children," Felicia said. "Do you think Cyril Wilding might be Mrs. Peck's baby? She's old enough, I would suspect."

"There's a good chance," Ginger admitted. "She came from the Battersea area, apparently." The only way they could know for sure is to ask Virginia Peck herself. Although, once one had lied about something for long enough, it maybe be hard for one to ever speak the truth about it.

"The question is," Ginger continued, "if Cyril Wilding is Virginia Peck's son, why would he want to kill Reginald Peck?"

CHAPTER TWENTY-ONE

hen Basil returned to Scotland Yard, he was surprised to find Laurence Winthrop waiting for him, especially so since he'd been less than cooperative at their last encounter.

"Come to my office," Basil said. "Would you like a cup of tea or coffee? My constable can round one up."

The solicitor accepted a wooden chair and balanced a briefcase on his lap. "No, thank you. I won't stay long."

"Very well," Basil said. Once they were both seated, he asked, "What can I do for you, Mr. Winthrop?"

Basil dearly hoped that the Peck family solicitor would make an announcement that would break the case wide open. These types of things occasionally happened, though more often in works of fiction.

"Chief Inspector Reed," the man said, his focus darting over Basil's shoulder. "Would you mind if I closed the door."

"Be my guest."

The man's spryness was evident in the quickness of his actions. "Family law can be quite trying," Winthrop admitted as he sat once more. "There's often so much secrecy between family members, and it's my job to keep confidences."

"But only to Mr. Peck, surely," Basil said. "He's the one who employed you."

"You are correct, of course. With him, I have to honour solicitor-client privilege."

"And now you find yourself torn. Loyalty to a client or break privilege and perhaps help solve his murder."

Winthrop removed a handkerchief from his pocket and wiped his brow. "Well, yes."

Basil felt a frisson of excitement. If only Winthrop wouldn't clam up.

"Chief Inspector Reed, I am here because I'm about to do that very thing, though it goes against every value I hold dear, and yet, I don't think it will help you very much."

"Why don't you let me be the judge of that," Basil said. "What do you know?"

"Three weeks before Mr. Peck died, he called me to his house."

"And?" Basil prompted. He hoped his impatience wasn't becoming apparent to Winthrop.

"Mr. Peck told me that he suspected that someone was trying to kill him."

Basil jerked back, startled by the pronouncement. "Did he say who?"

"No. Quite honestly, I thought he was growing delusional as a result of his disease. Certain medications can do that. I didn't really take his accusation seriously. I now deeply regret that. I know I should've told you this before."

Basil couldn't have agreed more, but it didn't help matters to dwell on what couldn't now be changed. "Please think back to the conversation, Mr. Winthrop. Did he mention any names, allude to anyone in the family or a member of staff, even in passing?"

Winthrop used his handkerchief to blow his nose. He looked at Basil with regret in his eyes. "I'm sorry. If he did, I don't remember it."

AFTER THE SOLICITOR HAD DEPARTED, Braxton knocked on Basil's office door and stuck his head in. "A message from your mother, sir." He put the hand-scribbled note on Basil's desk. "She wants you to ring her as soon as you're free."

"Yes, er, thank you, Constable."

Braxton stepped out, leaving Basil to fiddle nervously with the small piece of paper. Anna Reed was a force to be reckoned with, and if he didn't ring her soon, he would get an earful later, along with her well-practiced disparaging glare of disappointment.

Basil let out a frustrated grunt. He was a forty-one-year-old man, for crying out loud! Yet around his mother, he reverted to the shy youth who suffered silently under the weight of an overbearing parent.

His father wasn't much better, always siding with his wife. Truth be told, Basil had married Emelia, primarily, because his parents had been opposed to it. That followed his joining the army to spite them. And when he'd failed at that by being invalided out of service in the first year, he'd defied them by joining the Metropolitan Police.

A sigh of resignation escaped his lips. One might as well face the fire and get it over with. He lifted the receiver of the telephone that took up one corner of his desk and dialled. Before the call was even connected, he could hear his mother's voice out in the corridor.

"Just direct me to his office. I'll see for myself if he's here."

Basil hung the receiver back on the cradle and

stood, bracing himself as if for gale-force winds. In seconds, his mother and father blew through the door.

"Basil, darling!"

His mother wore a glamorous orange and peach day frock with an attached matching floral scarf. On her head sat a red turban hat with a large diamond-shaped glittering brooch pinned to the front. She swooped in and kissed him on each cheek like the French do, a habit she'd picked up on her travels.

"Mother, Father, what are you doing here?"

His father removed his expensive trilby from his head and held it against his well-made suit. "You seem rather impossible to get hold of," he said. "We had to take matters into our own hands."

"But I'm working."

"You work too much! You must have a little time to spare for your mother and father."

Basil knew the walls of his office were thin, and the tenor of his parents' voices would reverberate to the ears of his subordinates. This was a disastrous situation, and drastic measures were required.

"I can spare a few minutes," he said. "It's a lovely day. Would you fancy a stroll along the river?"

"Oh yes," his mother said. "I didn't want to mention it," she wrinkled her nose, "but it's rather stuffy in here."

Basil grabbed his hat and led the way outside,

uncomfortably aware of all the eyes in the Yard offices that followed their departure. Outside they crossed Victoria Embankment to the footpath and strolled along the muddied waters of the Thames. "You might as well get right to it," Basil said. With his parents, he would rather not beat around the bush to get to the point, a tactic the British were experts in.

"Get to what, darling?"

"You want to discuss Ginger and Scout, so get on with it."

"Well," his father huffed, "if you're going to be rude about it—"

"Not rude, Father, rather expedient." Basil pointed to his wristwatch. "I really am short on time."

"Very well," his mother said. "Ginger is a lovely woman, and a much better choice than Emelia—God rest her soul—but we thought she would give you children. And really, you haven't given it much time, have you? I've heard through the grapevine, *the grapevine,* Basil, that you're considering the adoption of a common waif."

"It's unconventional," Basil admitted.

"It's outrageous!"

"You're the man, Basil," his father said. "Tell her it's stuff and nonsense and have the boy removed."

"It's not as simple as that."

"Why?" his father insisted. "You're the man! Make her obey you or make her choose."

Before Basil could form words to express his shock, his mother added fuel to the fire. "You haven't been married very long. You could get your marriage annulled."

Basil stopped short. "Believe me, Mother, it's simply too late for something like that."

"Well, divorce then. The requirements could be arranged."

Basil stopped, appalled. Had his mother just suggested that he frame Ginger for adultery?

"You could find yourself a younger wife who knows her place," his father said. "One who values the home base and will give you blood heirs."

Clearly, his parents had spent time discussing such a repulsive scheme. "The two of you are unbelievable!"

"Are you really prepared to walk away from your fortune, Basil?" his mother asked.

"And if I were, what would you do with it?"

"There are my foolhardy nephews, of course," his father replied, "and we have several charities and organisations we support who will honour our names well into the future. But of course, we'd rather hand it to you and our grandchildren."

Basil's mother looked at him with eyes that pleaded for understanding. She wasn't evil, nor was his father.

They, like all parents, just wanted what they thought was best for their child. Basil couldn't blame them for that. And it wasn't like he hadn't wanted children, it had just never happened for him. Life was like that sometimes.

Even though his parents had often infuriated him over the years, Basil had to admit that they hadn't always been wrong. They had been right about Emelia.

"Basil?" his mother said.

Basil made a point of checking his wristwatch. "I really have to get back to work. We'll talk again later."

CHAPTER TWENTY-TWO

The first thing Ginger intended to do when she got back to the office with Felicia was to ring Basil. She wanted to convey her suspicions about Virginia and Cyril Wilding, but before she picked up the receiver to dial, she could hear Basil's voice in her head asking for proof.

So far, all she had was speculation. She needed something other than a hunch connecting the two. If Virginia had handed over an unwanted child to the Wildings in exchange for cash, it would explain how a girl without support could purchase the things she'd need to pretend to be someone she wasn't.

But if so, what was Cyril Wilding doing at the Pecks' house now? Had he learned of his natural mother's identity and now wanted money out of the deal?

It wasn't as if Cyril had been raised in poor conditions. His adoptive parents were solidly middle class.

"Ginger?"

Felicia's voice pulled Ginger out of her thoughts.

"Ginger? Come here for a moment."

Ginger found Felicia in the darkroom poring over the photographs she'd taken earlier that day.

"Oh, those do look better," Ginger said. "You can arrange to have them delivered to Mr. Soames."

"Yes, but have another look at my original photographs. I was comparing the two when I noticed this in the background of this shot. It's the least blurry of the bunch." Felicia handed Ginger a magnifying glass. "That man is carrying a tin of rat poison. Isn't that a coincidence?"

Ginger raised the magnifying glass over an image of a man leaving the shop. His chin was lowered, but enough of his face was revealed to suggest identity.

"Not only that," Ginger said, feeling a tingle of the thrill that comes with closing in on a case. "That's Cyril Wilding! It appears he was shopping at the very curiosity shop where Miss Soames works."

Now that Ginger had something substantial to give to Basil, she rang him without delay, but to her dismay, he wasn't in his office.

"Can I leave the chief inspector a message, Mrs. Reed?" the desk officer asked.

"Could you tell him to ring me at Hartigan House. I'm just leaving for there now and should arrive within twenty minutes."

"I shall do, madam."

Ginger placed her hat upon her bob and donned her gloves. "Keep the negatives in a safe place, Felicia," she said, "then deliver the photographs to Mr. Soames."

"All right. I'll meet you at the house later."

Ginger waved down a black taxicab and got in. How wonderful it would be if everyone could have a tiny telephone on their person so it wouldn't be so difficult to contact each other, but alas, that was the stuff of this new science fiction craze.

Outside, London landmarks passed by, but her mind was too busy on the Peck case to take it in.

Cyril Wilding purchased rat poison yesterday. Whatever for? He was a guest of Mrs. Peck's and not expected to deal with a rodent problem. However, according to Dr. Gupta, Mr. Peck had been poisoned. The exact nature of the poison would be discovered soon, but until then, one must assume the worst. A form of strychnine could be the culprit.

If so, perhaps Mr. Wilding planned to replace an empty canister before someone below stairs noticed.

Or, possibly, he meant to try to set someone else up by planting the poison in his or her room?

Again, motive was in question. Perhaps Mr. Wilding assumed Mrs. Peck was to inherit a mass sum, which he could then claim a right to as her son? As it stood, there wasn't a lot Virginia Peck could've given to Mr. Wilding without Mr. Peck being made aware.

Boss' cute little black and white face peered out from the sitting room window; his damp nose pressed against the glass.

Ginger pressed a hand to her heart as she walked through the wrought iron gates to the front door.

"Oh, Bossy, I've been gone too long!"

Inside, Boss ran to her, and Ginger scooped him up and pressed her face to his forehead whilst he kissed her neck.

"Such a good boy, aren't you? I shan't leave this house again today without you with me, I promise."

Boss calmed in her arms, and all was forgiven.

She passed Pips on her way to her study.

"Dear Pips, do you have any news for me? How have things gone in my absence?"

Ginger appreciated Pippins' intuitiveness. "Quite well, madam. Master Scout and Mr. Fulton appeared to get on rather well, though the youngster was eager to get back outside."

Ginger chuckled in relief. "I do believe he'd sleep in the stables if I let him."

A stack of unopened letters sat on her desk, and she sighed. "It never ends, does it, Boss?" She put her pet down, and he meandered to his bed by the unlit fireplace then gave Ginger a mournful look.

"It is a bit cool in here, isn't it? I fear it's about to rain."

She was just about to ring for someone to light the fire when Lizzie ducked in and curtsied. "Mr. Pippins thought you might like a fire?"

"Yes, thank you." Ginger hated to think of what she would ever do without Pippins and immediately dismissed the dreadful thought. To her, Pippins was an immortal, a fairy godfather—at least it was how she'd imagined him when she was a child, and she stubbornly held on to the belief.

"Is everything well in the house, Lizzie?" Ginger liked to keep her finger on the pulse of the lives of her staff. They were more than just people in her employ. Ginger considered them an extension of the Hartigan House family. "Are you well?"

Lizzie had begun adding coal and kindling to the hearth. "Yes, madam, thanks for asking. My mum has come down with a bad toothache, and my little sister has just damaged her arm in a fall, so there are two down who can't work at the moment. We're all very grateful to you for keeping me on."

"I'm sorry to hear things have been difficult at home."

"It's okay, madam, we manage. We always do."

Lizzie struck the match, and the welcome glow of fire grew.

"And how are things in the kitchen?" Ginger was concerned about Mrs. Beasley, who seemed to be struggling the most with adjusting to Scout's new status.

"Mrs. B. can be a bit rough around the edges at times. Best to just keep out of the way when she's like that." Lizzie shrugged. "The best you can anyway."

"Change is difficult for everyone," Ginger said. "Adjusting will come in time."

"Yes, madam."

Lizzie left, and Ginger took care of her correspondence. Most were invoices or confirmation notices regarding orders and events at Feathers & Flair. A few were invitations to charity events or high-society parties. One was a letter from Boston from her sister, Louisa. She'd save that one for later when she could put her feet up and enjoy it. Louisa's letters were always a source of entertainment.

Ginger gathered paper and her fountain pen and prepared to respond to the top item. Her eyes kept landing on the silent telephone as she willed Basil to call. What she thought she had discovered about Cyril Wilding might be relevant. Furthermore, if her theory was right, he could prove to be a danger to other members of the Peck household.

Ginger snatched up the receiver when her telephone rang, relieved to hear Basil's voice.

"Ginger, love," he said. "You rang?"

"Yes, Felicia and I made a couple of discoveries that may be of some interest to your case."

"Please proceed."

"Firstly, we tracked down Mr. Wildings birth records and it appears that he was adopted. Named after another child, recently deceased. He was born in Battersea."

"Virginia Peck came from that area," Basil said. "Are you suggesting Mr. Wilding is her son?"

"It would explain how she got the money needed to create a new life for herself."

"Indeed."

"And secondly, Felicia followed a lady in regard to a separate case, one of ours, and whilst taking photographs happened to snap an image of Cyril Wilding."

"Really? How coincidental."

"Rather. But here's the intriguing bit. Mr. Wilding had made a purchase at the shop Felicia had been watching. Rat poison."

"Indeed," Basil said. "That is rather interesting, but hardly proof of anything other than he'd discovered a rodent problem somewhere. Now if Dr. Gupta's reports confirm the poison type, well then, I'll have to bring Mr. Wilding in for a chat. Please tell Felicia, she's done a good job."

CHAPTER TWENTY-THREE

*L*ater that night, Ginger did something she'd never done before in her life. She tucked Scout into bed.

She had had the room especially decorated and furnished in a way she hoped would please a young boy. Wallpaper with sailing boats, a table with a train set, and from the ceiling hung a model aeroplane. Against the wall was a wooden bookshelf painted white and filled with books Ginger had ordered from Hatchards bookshop.

Already small for his size, Scout looked even smaller in the large bed dotted with grand fluffy pillows.

"How was your day?" she asked him.

"Good."

"Did you get along with Mr. Fulton?"

"Yeah. 'E's nice, I guess, though he's really keen about learnin'."

Ginger chuckled. "I'm happy to hear it."

"Do I have to do learnin' every day?"

"I'm sure Mr. Fulton would like Sundays off."

Ginger studied the collection of books she'd recently ordered now propped upright with spines outward on the shelves. "Would you like to read a book together?" she asked.

"I dunno 'ow to read."

"Are you sure about that? You've been studying your letters for a while now."

"I'm learnin' them in my 'ead."

"Perhaps we can take turns," Ginger said confidently. "How about *The Swiss Family Robinson?*" Ginger removed the volume. "It has a lot of adventure."

"Okay."

Ginger sat in the chair, propped the book under the light and began.

"*Chapter One. The tempest had raged for six days, and on the seventh seemed to increase. The ship had been so far driven from its course, that no one on board knew where we were. Everyone was exhausted with fatigue and watching. The shattered vessel began to leak in many places, the oaths of the sailors were changed to prayers, and each thought only how to save his own life.*"

She glanced over the edge of the book pages, pleased that the opening paragraph already had Scout's attention, a tribute to Johann David Wyss' talents.

"'Children,' said I to my terrified boys, who were clinging round me, 'God can save us if he will. To him, nothing is impossible; but if he thinks it good to call us to him, let us not murmur; we shall not be separated.'

"My excellent wife dried her tears, and from that moment became more tranquil. We knelt down to pray—"

"Missus Mum?"

"Yes, Scout?"

"Sumtimes Lizzie makes me pray."

"That's good. We can pray together when we've finished here if you like?"

"I fink it would be nice."

"Okay." Ginger smiled, then continued her recitation.

"We rose from our knees strengthened to bear the afflictions that hung over us. Suddenly we heard amid the roaring of the waves the cry of 'Land! Land!' At that moment, the ship struck on a rock; the concussion threw us down. We heard a loud cracking as if the vessel was parting asunder; we felt that we were aground, and heard the captain cry, in a tone of despair, 'We are lost! —'"

"Missus Mum, it's scary."

"Too scary?"

"No! Keep reading."

"*I went on deck, and was instantly thrown down, and wet through by a huge sea; a second followed. I struggled boldly with the waves, and succeeding in keeping myself up, when I saw, with terror, the extent of our wretchedness—*"

"Missus Mum?"

"Yes, Scout?"

"I am afraid."

"Should I stop reading?"

"Not of the book."

"Oh, of what then?"

"I'm afraid I'll never be posh, Missus." His lower lip quivered. "I'm not like you and the mister."

"Oh, Scout," Ginger's chest ached for the lad. "You don't need to be posh. Just be you."

"But you want to change me. How I talk, how I dress, this fancy room."

"You don't like your new things?"

"I do, I do. Just, I'm afraid of getting too used to it. You'll change your mind one day, you will."

"No, Scout," Ginger said firmly. "I promise you I won't, I give you my word, and my word is my bond." There was a look in Scout's eyes, a flash of maturity that gave Ginger a brief glimpse into the future, a possible future, and she shivered at the thought that maybe it wasn't Scout's fear she might tire of him, but Ginger's fear he might one day tire of her.

Scout sniffed and, before Ginger could offer a handkerchief, wiped his nose on his sleeve.

"You must know that I'm very fond of you, Scout," Ginger said gently. "Would it frighten you terribly if I said that I love you with a mother's love?"

Scout's eyes widened, glistening with emotion. "I luv ya too, Mum."

Ginger's heart nearly burst, aware that Scout had dropped the prefix, "missus".

"How wonderful for us both. Now, shall I keep reading, or do you want to take a turn?"

Scout snuggled under his covers. "You can keep reading. I'll take a turn next time."

"Very well, but you must promise."

"I promise."

Ginger continued, and when she got to the end of the chapter, she closed the book.

"Aw, Mum, is that all?"

"That's all for now."

"Okay. Good night."

"What about your evening prayers?"

"That's why I got my eyes closed."

"I see. Do you still want to say them together?"

"Nah, I fink I'm too old for that. I'm fine now."

"Yes, right. Very well, then. Good night, Scout." She kissed him gently on the head before turning out the light and closing the door halfway.

Ginger's emotions were mixed. She triumphed in what she felt was a victory with Scout but also berated herself for waiting so long to take over from Lizzie. Her maid had been caring for Scout primarily for almost a year, since Ginger had taken him in off the streets, and had done all the motherly things Ginger, in her new role now, was meant to do. Ginger knew she often treated Scout as though he were younger than he actually was, and it grieved her to think that she had missed his childhood.

CHAPTER TWENTY-FOUR

The next morning Ginger was dealing with correspondence in her study at Hartigan House when Pippins interrupted with a quiet knock.

"Madam, a Mrs. Northcott is here to see you."

"Really?" Ginger sat back in surprise. "Please show her in."

Moments later, Mrs. Northcott sat in one of the wooden chairs that faced Ginger's desk.

"I'm sorry to bother you at home, Mrs. Reed," she said, "but I rang your office and Miss Gold informed me that you'd yet to come in. I thought I'd take a chance, hoping to catch you and came post haste."

Mrs. Northcott was clearly agitated.

"It's quite all right, Mrs. Northcott," Ginger said soothingly. "What have you discovered?"

Mrs. Northcott removed an envelope from her

handbag. "This." She handed over the opened envelope and its contents.

"My maid found it in Virginia's desk. I'm afraid I required her to do some snooping on my behalf. I just couldn't rest thinking she may have killed my father."

Ginger's curiosity was whetted. The envelope was addressed to Mrs. Peck at Eaton Square. She unfolded the single sheet of paper and read.

Dear Mrs. Peck,

We were acquainted when you were known as Miss Robinson. Actually, acquainted is the wrong word. You see, I've recently learned I am your son. I want you to know that I hold no animosity towards you for the exchange you made with the couple I call Mum and Dad, but now that your circumstances have clearly changed, I hope you wouldn't mind meeting. All confidences will be kept. My request to see you is merely a matter of curiosity. Nature calls a child and mother together. I hope you feel it too.

With warmest regards,

Cyril Wilding.

Ginger's suspicions had been correct. She glanced up at Mrs. Northcott's stern countenance.

"This is proof that Virginia lied to my father," she said. "If the truth about her sordid past had been known, Papa would never have married her."

This might or might not have been accurate as

Ginger knew that love was a powerful force and rather blind when the bearer wanted it to be. She answered kindly, "It's proof that Cyril Wilding believes her to be his mother, that's all."

"If it's not true, then why is he still in residence in my home?"

"Even if it is true, it's not proof of murder." Though Ginger had to admit that the letter combined with Felicia's photograph was compelling.

"It's proof of motive," Mrs. Northcott said. "What if Papa found out? What if he was about to change his will to cut Virginia out of it?"

The possibility had crossed Ginger's mind. "Do you think Virginia killed her husband?"

"I do," Mrs. Northcott said. "And I want you to prove it."

Ginger blinked back. "Are you saying you want to employ me in an official capacity?"

"I do."

"But the police are actively on the case."

"Do you know how many murders per year go unsolved, Mrs. Reed? Here in London? Many, so forgive me if my faith in the police isn't what it should be."

"Very well. I do have to point out then that just yesterday you were convinced Mr. Wilding was our killer."

"I stand by the possibility. In fact, it wouldn't shock me to discover that the two of them worked together to finish Papa off." Mrs. Northcott's voice cracked, and she glanced away.

"I'll do what I can to help, Mrs. Northcott, and as much as I work diligently for each of my clients, I must follow where the evidence leads, even if it goes in a direction not to my client's favour. Are you prepared for that, Mrs. Northcott?"

Ginger's proclamation caught Mrs. Northcott off guard. Her lips worked as she mentally processed the possible outcomes.

"I think, Mrs. Reed, that perhaps I need a little more time to think things through. You're quite right that the police are at work, and with you working so closely with the chief inspector anyway, it seems a needless doubling of efforts."

Mrs. Northcott got to her feet, blushing with unexplained sheepishness. "I'm sorry for this intrusion. I can find my way out."

Ginger sat back feeling nonplussed. She'd unnerved Mrs. Northcott with her little speech, and couldn't help but wonder why.

CHAPTER TWENTY-FIVE

Ginger rang Scotland Yard and was pleased that Basil was available to take her call. "Mrs. Northcott was here to see me," she explained. "She'd discovered something of interest."

Ginger shared Mrs. Northcott's findings.

Basil let out a low whistle. "Do you have the letter?"

Ginger had made sure to leave it on the desk, but with Mrs. Northcott's sudden need to flee, she'd forgotten to retrieve the envelope anyway. Ginger answered, "I do."

"I'm sending officers to collect Mr. Wilding. I believe it's time we had a chat. Would you mind terribly bringing me the letter and the photograph?"

"Not at all," Ginger said. She had had every intention of doing so, even if Basil had suggested sending an officer round to collect them.

Boss lifted his head and watched as Ginger put on her hat and gloves. "I did promise I wouldn't leave you, didn't I?"

Boss stretched and strolled to her side.

"Very well, come along." Ginger slid the envelope with Cyril's letter to Virginia into her handbag. The incriminating photograph was already tucked inside.

The tapping of Ginger's shoes along with the light clicking of Boss' nails on the marble floor reverberated through the hall. Pippins, as usual, suddenly appeared.

"It's the shoes that give us away, isn't it, Pips?" Ginger said with a laugh. "One needs slippers if one is to sneak anything past you."

Pippins bowed, grinning softly as he did so.

Ginger had become quite adept at backing the motorcar out of the garage. There was one slight dent on the rear bumper, barely noticeable, and Ginger chose not to think about it. Boss was always up for a trip in the Crossley and pushed his nose out of the opened window.

Ginger felt a tingle of excitement as she pulled into the parking area behind the two Scotland Yard buildings. Had they got their man? Was Cyril Wilding the killer? Or might it be Virginia in the end?

Constable Braxton greeted her at the front desk.

"Hello, Mrs. Reed. You've brought your dog, I see?"

Boss was safely in her arms. "He's very well trained and won't make a peep. Besides he's been here before."

"Ah, before I came on the scene. It's not a problem with me, Mrs. Reed." His lips twitched before continuing. "Might I ask after your family?"

Ginger held in the grin that threatened. The dashing constable surely wasn't asking after Ambrosia. "Everyone is quite well, thank you. Miss Gold in particular."

Constable Braxton's complexion flushed red. "I've been caught out. Do pass on my regards."

"I shall."

Basil had briefed her a little on Constable Braxton's background. He came from a good family and had been educated at Winchester.

Ambrosia might come around to another officer of the law in the family if it weren't for the belief that a true gentleman didn't *have* to work. It was only because Basil came from money that she overlooked the work he did at Scotland Yard.

Ginger found Basil waiting for her in his office.

"Darling," she said, giving him a respectable kiss on the cheek.

"Please sit down," Basil said.

Ginger claimed one of the empty wooden chairs

and allowed Boss to get comfortable on her lap. She then removed the envelope and the photograph from her Coco Chanel handbag—Ginger thought the interlocking Cs were a clever touch—and pushed them across Basil's desk.

"Cyril Wilding has been apprehended and is in an interrogation room. I can't let you come in, Ginger, Scott will be present, along with Wilding's solicitor."

"Oh, boo."

"But I shall instruct Braxton to leave the door open a crack whilst he guards the hall. I can't help it if you wander by."

"Love, you are the best!"

CHAPTER TWENTY-SIX

*G*inger had done her fair share of spying on people without their awareness during her work in the Great War. Generally, in those days, the stakes had been far higher, and her life weighed in the balance should she have ever been caught. Despite knowing she was safe, she sometimes suffered a chill of nerves when she did anything that reminded her of those times.

At twenty-four, Cyril Wilding was the same age as many of the German soldiers she'd encountered on the continent. So young, yet with staggering degrees of authority.

She let the thought go and focused on the interview.

"I don't understand why I'm here," Mr. Wilding said tersely. "Surely, your men could've asked me whatever it is you want to know without creating a humiliating scene."

"I do apologise for any social discomfort you experienced," Basil said. He sat at the table opposite Mr. Wilding whilst Sergeant Scott, an older, heavyset officer wearing a standard black police uniform, sat across from Mr. Wilding's legal representative. "However," Basil continued, "it's proper form here at Scotland Yard to interview potential murder suspects on our premises."

"Murder suspect? Me? You can't be serious."

"We take every murder investigation seriously."

"You're referring to Mr. Peck, I'm assuming. I barely knew the man. I think we said a mere handful of words to one another. Why on earth would I kill him?"

Basil opened a folder that sat on the table in front of him and removed a photograph. Ginger knew it was a copy of the one Felicia had taken.

"This was snapped the other day. It is you, is it not?"

Cyril Wilding's youthful brow furrowed deeply. "I say, who's been following me? I didn't give permission for this."

"They were actually shooting a photograph of this young lady here," Basil said pointing. "Your image was captured quite by accident. I'd like to point out the item in your hand." Basil slid a magnifying glass towards Mr. Wilding. "You may use that if you think it will be helpful."

Mr. Wilding picked up the magnifying glass and stared at the photograph. From her spot by the door, Ginger could see the young man losing colour.

Mr. Wilding laid the magnifying glass down. "It's rat poison. What of it?"

"Well, Mr. Peck was poisoned. And you've been a guest of Mrs. Peck's for long enough to have committed the deed."

Mr. Wilding's solicitor shook his head. "You don't have to comment."

"I will anyway," Mr. Wilding said, "because I didn't do it."

Basil pressed on. "Why did you buy rat poison?"

Mr. Wilding stared at his fingernails. "There are mice in my room. I didn't want to embarrass my hostess, so I thought I'd just take matters into my own hands."

"Indeed?" Basil said.

"Besides," Mr. Wilding continued, "why would I want to kill anyone?"

"Ah yes, motive," Basil said. "Means and opportunity aren't enough; one must also determine why."

Basil presented the letter.

Cyril Wilding's neck flushed red as awareness

gripped him. "Where did you get this? This is personal correspondence, and you have no right to it."

"Regardless, Mr. Wilding, it presents a plausible motive. Firstly, you discover the identity of the woman who brought you into this world, and then you find out that she has money that you feel you have a right to. Only, you discover she can't gain access to the funds. Then it occurs to you that as Mr. Peck's wife, she would most likely inherit a significant part of Mr. Peck's estate. It must've been quite a disappointment for you at the reading of the will."

Cyril hit the table with his fist. "I did not kill Mr. Peck. And these documents don't prove anything. I simply wanted to locate my mother, and it turns out she was wondering about me as well. It's been a joyous reunion. At least, it was until this deplorable turn of events."

"Mr. Wilding, why did you purchase the poison?"

For the first time, Mr. Wilding appeared frightened. "Someone asked me to."

"Who?"

"I'd rather not say."

"Because your answer will incriminate the person who made the request?"

Mr. Wilding got his courage back. "Are you charging me with murder? Do it or let me go."

"If you insist," Basil said. "Mr. Cyril Wilding, you

are arrested on the suspicion of the murder of Mr. Reginald Peck."

Sergeant Scott handcuffed Mr. Wilding, and Ginger knew it was her signal to leave before either Mr. Wilding or his solicitor spotted her. She winked at Constable Braxton who remained at his post, a clear look of confusion on his face.

CHAPTER TWENTY-SEVEN

Ginger was stunned to run into Virginia Peck in the Scotland Yard waiting area.

"Mrs. Peck?"

The new widow, dressed head to toe in black, returned the look of surprise. "Mrs. Reed? What are you—oh, yes, you assist your husband."

Ginger kept her eyes soft as she drew closer. "I'm sorry about Mr. Wilding."

Mrs. Peck's chin jutted upwards in defiance. "I hope they haven't arrested him."

"I'm afraid they have."

"Well," Mrs. Peck said with a derisive huff. "Scotland Yard's about to find itself pretty red-faced shortly."

Ginger felt her defences rise. "Why do you say that?"

"Because I killed my husband. I'm here to confess."

Oh mercy.

"I'm afraid they have compelling evidence against Mr. Wilding," Ginger said.

"Purely circumstantial, I'm sure." Mrs. Peck side-stepped Ginger. "Officer?"

Constable Braxton lifted his gaze. "Yes?"

"I'm here to turn myself in. I'm a murderer. Please take me away."

Ginger cast a disbelieving glance at Basil, who'd just entered the room in time to hear Virginia Peck's last declaration.

"Mrs. Peck," he said. "Please accompany me."

Virginia Peck, with all the dignity the Peck name commanded, kept her head high and followed Basil into his office. Ginger didn't wait to be invited to join them and stepped in behind her husband as if she had every right to do it. Mrs. Peck sat at the chair in front of Basil's desk, and Ginger claimed the remaining empty one.

"I thought you'd be putting me behind bars, Chief Inspector," Mrs. Peck said. "Or is this just a formality."

Basil settled into his seat on the opposite side of the table. "Let's have a chat first, shall we?"

"Very well."

Basil exhaled as he leaned in. "We know about your familial relationship to Mr. Wilding."

"Yes, he's my son. I expected it might come to light as a result of your investigation."

"Why didn't you mention it before?" Ginger asked.

Mrs. Peck cast a tired look Ginger's way. "I didn't see the relevance at the time."

Ginger nodded, then added, "A mother and child bond can be powerful, even if a lot of time and distance has separated them."

"Surprisingly strong," Mrs. Peck admitted.

"And that's why you're making a false claim to killing your husband," Basil stated. "It's foolishness on your part, Mrs. Peck. You can get charged for wasting police time, and it wouldn't help your son's case."

"Except that it's true," Mrs. Peck insisted. "I did kill Reginald."

"In that case," Basil said, "what was your motive? You were well aware, more so than anyone, that your husband was terminally ill and didn't have long to live."

"I worried about his mental upheaval—his mood swings were unpredictable and his personality changes disturbing—that he might do something drastic in his last days and cut me out of his will. I've grown accustomed to a certain lifestyle—one I couldn't maintain on my own without funding from my husband's estate."

"Yet, here you are, ready to walk away from all those comforts," Ginger said.

"Cyril is the only thing that could drive me to it. I couldn't bear to see him pay for a crime I'd committed. Any parent would be vile to do so."

"We have evidence proving that Mr. Wilding purchased poison," Basil said. "Why would he do that?"

Mrs. Peck hesitated, then answered, "Because I asked him to buy it."

Cyril Wilding did say he bought it for someone, Ginger thought, and if true, covering for Mrs. Peck would be a good reason why he didn't want to say for whom.

"What kind of poison did you ask him to buy?" Basil asked.

Mrs. Peck's mouth opened, and when she failed to come up with an answer, she snapped her lips closed.

"Mrs. Peck," Basil said with a sigh, "I can't arrest you."

"Why on earth not? I'm confessing!"

"But it's a false confession." Basil leaned over the table, fingers clasped, and stared back at Mrs. Peck with empathy in his eyes. "I'm truly sorry for all the grief you've encountered in these last days."

"But Cyril is innocent."

"If so, a jury shall come to that conclusion as well."

Mrs. Peck left in a huff.

"Poor lady," Ginger said. "First losing a husband, then a long-lost son so soon after just finding him again. Such a sad tale."

CHAPTER TWENTY-EIGHT

Ginger called in at Feathers & Flair after leaving Basil at Scotland Yard. With so much chaos and anxiety in the investigation, Ginger found the relative calm and order of her dress shop soothing.

Her peace of mind was soon disrupted by the entrance of the next potential customer. Ginger resisted gulping when she spotted her mother-in-law walking towards her. Instead, she forced a smile.

"Mrs. Reed," Ginger said as the lady approached. "How wonderful to see you."

"Hello, Ginger," Mrs. Reed said coolly. She glanced slowly about the shop and took everything in.

Ginger refused to be disquieted.

"It's nice," Mrs. Reed finally said. "I've never been in before."

"It is rather new." Ginger had only opened the shop the previous autumn. "And you've been away."

"Yes," Mrs. Reed said, making a show of pulling off her gloves. "It's quite astounding how much things can change whilst one is away." Her gaze locked on Ginger. "Take you, for instance, and your marriage to my son."

"That wasn't as sudden as it might appear," Ginger said, feeling defensive. "We knew each other for a while before—"

"Before Emelia died, I know." Mrs. Reed ran fingers through the silk scarves on display, her eyes glancing toward Madame Roux and the customer she was engaged with across the room.

"Ginger, darling, we're related now, and I would like to get to know you better. Perhaps you could get away for a cup of tea?"

"I'd be happy to make some," Ginger said. "My office is just around the corner, and we can be alone there."

Ginger thought that if Felicia happened to be ensconced at the Lady Gold Investigations office an excuse to relieve her would be warranted, but the office was locked when they got there. Ginger produced a key and opened the door.

"What kind of office is this?"

"It's my investigation office." Ginger watched Mrs.

Reed's response as she offered her a chair. Surely, Basil had mentioned it?

"You'll have to explain," Mrs. Reed said, her brow furrowed. "What is it exactly that you do?"

"I help my clients find things," Ginger said. "People, information, lost items. Now if you'll excuse me for a moment, I'll put the kettle on."

Ginger willed the gas ring to hurry up and heat the kettle. The sooner she had the tea made, the sooner they could drink it and be finished with this uncomfortable attempt at faux mother-daughter intimacy.

She returned with a tray. "Milk, Mrs. Reed?"

"Yes, please."

Ginger poured milk into each of their teacups then added the tea. Mrs. Reed helped herself to sugar and stirred.

"You're quite unconventional," Mrs. Reed said, "for an English lady, with your businesses and modern outlook. It's your American influence, I'd say."

Ginger didn't bite. "You're rather unconventional yourself. World traveller, adventurer."

Mrs. Reed sipped her tea, paused to mentally assess it, and apparently finding it acceptable, said, "I suppose, in that way we're alike."

"I hope we'll get on," Ginger said sincerely.

"As do I. I hope we're friendly enough to discuss a rather sensitive subject."

Aha. The real reason for Mrs. Reed's desire to cosy up. Ginger braced herself.

Mrs. Reed leaned in and lowered her voice as if that would reduce the measure of her impertinence. "Harry and I are hoping to be grandparents one day, Ginger. Basil is our only means."

"I don't believe that's part of God's plans for us," Ginger said stiffly. In the five years she'd been married to Daniel, she'd never conceived, and it appeared the same pattern was shaping up with Basil.

Mrs. Reed straightened, her brightly painted lips working. "He must've known since you and your late husband never conceived."

"I kept nothing from Basil. Apparently, the matter of having children or not didn't weigh heavily with him, since it didn't keep him from proposing."

Mrs. Reed flicked her fingers. "Men don't think with their heads when they're in that state. If only I'd been here—"

"Then what?" Ginger demanded. She set her teacup down. "You'd have talked Basil out of getting married?"

Mrs. Reed's lips twitched as she forced a smile. "It's not that you're not lovely, Ginger, and you're perfectly acceptable wife material in every other way."

Ginger blinked at the backhanded compliment.

Mrs. Reed misread Ginger's silence as capitulation.

"We know about your intention to adopt, er, that boy," she said.

Ginger's heartbeat quickened, and she had to work to control her breath lest she betray the anger she felt. "Yes, the plans are in motion."

Mrs. Reed clicked her tongue. "Such a big step. Mr. Reed and I really wish you'd spoken to us before taking steps to go forward."

The forced smile on Ginger's face tightened. For one thing, she and Basil had had no way of knowing when the Reeds planned to return to London, and secondly, she and Basil didn't need their approval.

"Yes, well, we're quite far into it now." Ginger said. England's new laws regarding adoption were still in process, but Ginger's emotional commitment was unwavering.

"Such a shame."

"Why do you say that?" Ginger asked, feeling exasperated.

"Mr. Reed and I are obligated now to write Basil out of the will."

Ginger's jaw dropped. "I can't see what that has to do with anything."

"If something should happen to Basil, our estate can't be left to a street urchin. The idea of it is ridiculous."

"But, you yourself adopted a needy child, *Anna,*"

Ginger said. If Anna Reed was determined to talk about Ginger's personal life to such a degree, she would put things on an equal footing by using her Christian name.

Anna pinched her lips, then pressed on. "Yes, but we had Basil to hand our fortune to. Elias would've been adequately cared for, certainly, but our natural heir would inherit the family fortune. And, without an heir, we shall pass our assets on to Mr. Reed's brother's children. We can't risk our estate being handed down to that boy, even if we're not alive to see it."

"But you can do the same thing as you planned to do before," Ginger said, thoroughly alarmed. "And bypass Basil's adopted son?"

Mrs. Reed clicked her tongue. "What would people think of us then?"

"What will they think of you now?"

Mrs. Reed stood and smoothed out her frock. "Obviously, no one would know besides us, now, Ginger. Please, if you love Basil, do consider dropping the adoption for his sake."

CHAPTER TWENTY-NINE

If she loved Basil?

How dare Anna Reed insinuate otherwise. *How dare she!*

By the time Ginger returned to Hartigan House,
she'd reined in her emotions. People with high social
standing had a different way of viewing the world.
Everything was a possession to be managed, organised,
and invested—even one's children and future grandchildren. She couldn't blame Anna for being the
person she was. The question was, how could Ginger
live with such backward thinking? And even more
importantly, what did Basil *really* think?

Ginger parked the Crossley in the garage, took a
moment to check the bumper—oh mercy, a definite
dent. She'd bumped against a lamppost as she'd sped
away from her shop, which meant another trip to the

garage. They were sure to tire of her, though she was good for business, she supposed.

Scout played with Boss in the back garden, and the sight of them lifted Ginger's spirits. Matters of the heart were beyond the control of people like Henry and Anna Reed. She stopped to pat Scout on the head and give Boss a scrub behind the ears.

"You lot are having fun," Ginger said.

"Boss is really clever, Missus Mum. I've taught him to play hide and seek. Just watch." Scout turned his attention to Boss. "Sit, boy. Now, wait." Boss stayed on his haunches as instructed, but the excited dog simply could not control the shimmying of his tail stump.

"Wait. Wait. Wait," Scout said as his voice grew quieter with his distance. He squatted behind a patio chair near the French door of the morning room then called out, "Come and find me, Boss."

Boss made a show of searching every nook and cranny, but Ginger was certain her intelligent pet knew exactly where Scout was. Ginger laughed. It was part of the game.

Moments later, Boss came across Scout's hiding place.

"You found me!" Scout stood and made his declaration once more. "See, he's really clever!"

"He is," Ginger said, her smile even brighter. "And so are you for teaching him such a complicated game."

Inside, Ginger found Basil waiting for her in the sitting room.

"Your mother came to see me at Feathers & Flair today," Ginger said.

Basil held out a glass of brandy. "You could use this, then, I gather."

"Yes, thank you, love." Ginger settled onto the settee beside him, knocked off her shoes, and curled up. "It's been a long day, and your mother wasn't exactly the icing on the cake."

"I hope she didn't unsettle you too much."

"She's not very happy about Scout. She says they'll cut you out of their will." Ginger watched Basil's countenance carefully. The corner of his eye twitched, something he did when he was trying to keep his expression emotionally blank. When he didn't respond, she continued, "They wouldn't really go through with it, do you think?"

Basil swallowed a rather large gulp of brandy. "You never can tell with my parents. They don't exactly play by the rules."

"And yet, they want you to."

"It's not fair, I know."

"So, what are we to do?"

Basil took another sip from his brandy glass then said, "Did she say why she didn't want us to adopt Scout?"

"She doesn't want their money to get into his hands." Ginger eyed Basil narrowly. "But you knew that already."

"Yes, I had a visit from my parents today, as well."

"And what did you tell them."

"I didn't have a chance to tell them anything. They were quite busy doing all the talking."

Ginger faced him and made him look her in the eye. "What did they say?"

"Much the same as the message you got, I imagine." He placed a palm on Ginger's arm and conjured a grin. "Let's not worry about them, right now. If we're lucky, they'll go on another long trip soon."

Ginger appreciated Basil's attempt at humour, but couldn't help feeling rankled by his parents' intrusion into their lives in this manner.

Boss nosed his way into the room, and immediately claimed a space by Ginger's feet, and she appreciated the distraction. She toed her pet playfully. He licked her foot in response, and she couldn't help but giggle. "That tickles."

Ready to play, Boss flipped onto his back, but Ginger noticed that, despite Basil's casual demeanour, the subject of Scout was a sticky one, and perhaps it would be wise to leave further discussion until the morning, after they'd both had a good night's sleep and a strong cup of coffee.

"What did you think about that performance by Virginia Peck?" she said, changing the subject.

"I'm perplexed why she would do something so drastic as to confess to a murder she didn't commit. She must know she could hang for it."

"It's quite natural for a parent to want to rescue their child," Ginger said.

"Or she may only hope to create a question in the minds of the jury."

"Reasonable doubt?"

"Our case against Wilding isn't strong," Basil said. "If Virginia Peck's counsel could convince half the members of the jury that they might have the wrong man, the conviction would be overturned."

"And they'd both be acquitted," Ginger said, understanding. Unconsciously, she twisted the red curl that rested on her cheek with her finger. "There's nothing you can do about it, darling," Ginger said. "You did your job, now it's the court's turn to do theirs."

"Unless—"

Ginger knew what Basil was going to say, because she was thinking it herself. She finished his sentence, "Mrs. Peck is telling the truth."

"And I just arrested an innocent man."

The telephone rang, and Ginger could hear Pippins' reserved voice answer the call. She expected the knock on the sitting room door when it came.

"Sorry to interrupt, but the telephone is for you, sir."

Basil excused himself, and Ginger finished the last of her brandy. Something told her to put on her shoes. No one rang for Basil at night if it wasn't a matter of urgency.

Unless it was one of Basil's parents? Perhaps they'd come to their senses and had rung to apologise. One could hope.

But that hope was dashed when Basil returned with a hard look of consternation on his face.

"What is it, darling?"

"I've got another body," Basil said.

Oh mercy.

"Where?"

"Eaton Square again. It's Virginia Peck."

CHAPTER THIRTY

Ginger hadn't expected to be back at the Peck residence so soon, and certainly not under these grim circumstances.

Sergeant Scott and Constable Braxton were already present when Basil and Ginger arrived. Dr. Gupta got there a few minutes later.

The body of Virginia Peck was found in her bedroom in a red velvet high-backed chair. Sergeant Scott had the Yard's French Furet camera aimed at the crime scene and took photographs that filled the air with flash-pan smoke whilst Constable Braxton tagged evidence. With his thumb and forefinger, Dr. Gupta opened the lids of the corpse's eyes, then tested the dexterity of the jaw and limbs.

"Hello again, Dr. Gupta," Ginger said.

"Good evening, Mrs. Reed. Chief Inspector."

"Dr. Gupta," Basil said. "What do we have here?"

"Rigour has yet to set in. She's been dead less than four hours. No apparent wounding."

On a tray was a pot of tea, and a newly opened packet of tea. A teacup, half empty, sat on a matching saucer.

"Poison again?" Basil asked.

The pathologist mumbled, "Quite possibly."

"Strychnine?" Ginger said, thinking of the rat poison Mr. Wilding had purchased.

Dr. Gupta stared up at Ginger, but his eyes were unfocused as he considered her question. "With strychnine, I'd expect to see evidence of reflexive convulsions, which I don't see here."

"Any idea of what the poison might be?" Basil asked. "Have you heard from the laboratory yet?"

"It's only been two days," Dr. Gupta replied, "and I've heard nothing other than the liquid in Mr. Peck's stomach contents hasn't confirmed the presence of anything native to England."

"Do you think it might be a poison from a foreign source?" Basil asked

"We'll soon find out," Dr. Gupta said, "if all goes well."

Ginger took in the details of the scene. A large, fashionably decorated room with ornately carved wooden furniture, a luxuriously thick rose petal quilt, and a dressing table by the window.

Spotting a piece of brown paper in the near-empty rubbish bin, Ginger picked it up with her gloved hand. "This looks like parcel paper." It was squared in the corners on one end. "It's addressed to Virginia Peck. I wonder what it was?" Ginger searched for something in the room that looked new, that could've fitted inside.

Basil squinted as he read the postmark. "It was sent from London."

Ginger had a recollection. "That first time we tracked down Mr. Winthrop, he was heading to the post office. If I remember correctly, the parcel he sent was that same shape and size."

Basil turned to one of the constables. "Please ring Mr. Laurence Winthrop and ask him to meet me. And take this tea to the lab for testing."

"Yes, sir."

Only a few hours ago, Mrs. Peck had demanded she be arrested for Mr. Peck's murder. Ginger couldn't help thinking that Mrs. Peck might still be alive had Basil done as she'd asked. But then, possibly it might've been Cyril Wilding's body they were viewing now.

If there was a silver lining, it was an alibi for Mr. Wilding. He couldn't have possibly killed his mother and was therefore potentially innocent of Mr. Peck's murder.

"Braxton, I need a list of everyone who was known to be on the premises this evening," Basil said, "starting with the staff. I want to know who brought Mrs. Peck her tea this evening."

"I have it already, sir. The only members of the staff in the house this evening are the two who reside on the premises, Mrs. McCullagh, the housekeeper, and Mr. Murphy, the butler. Mrs. McCullagh is waiting in the dining room. Mr. Murphy is apparently in the conservatory. I'm on my way to fetch him now."

"No, that's all right," Basil said. "I'd like to see the conservatory again. I can speak to Mr. Murphy there."

Mrs. McCullagh looked unwell, Ginger thought. Her skin seemed heavy and her normally proud stance, broken.

"My sympathies," Ginger said. Losing Mrs. Peck could likely mean the loss of employment for Mrs. McCullagh unless the Peck offspring kept her on. From Ginger's observation, the housekeeper's loyalties lay with Mrs. Peck and in opposition to Mr. Peck's children, and so the lady found herself on the wrong side of things now.

Ginger and Basil seated themselves opposite the housekeeper.

"I know this is difficult," Basil said, "so we'll be quick. Did you take Mrs. Peck her tea this evening?"

Mrs. McCullagh shook her head. "Mrs. Peck preferred to brew the tea herself. She has a gas ring in her room for that purpose."

"Was it possible that someone else may have tampered with the teapot?" Basil asked.

"Not whilst the pot was in my possession. It's quite possible that someone may have entered Mrs. Peck's room after I'd left, though it would've been unseemly. Mrs. Peck was already in her night clothes."

"Did Mrs. Peck receive a small parcel in today's post?" Ginger asked.

Mrs. McCullagh looked at her blankly before shrugging. "You'd have to ask Mr. Murphy about that."

"I understand he's in the conservatory," Basil said.

"I believe so," Mrs. McCullagh said, "But it's not my place to monitor Mr. Murphy's comings and goings."

"Is that a usual thing for him to do in the evenings?"

"I don't go up there, but Mr. Murphy helped Mr. Peck with his botany obsession often. You could say he became Mr. Peck's legs and feet in these last months."

"Did you and Mrs. Peck get on?" Basil asked.

"Mrs. Peck was a demanding lady, wanting everything to be perfect, including me, but I could've done worse, I suppose."

BASIL SOUGHT the butler on the rooftop of the Peck residence whilst Ginger stayed with Mrs. McCullagh. They agreed that the housekeeper shouldn't be left alone. Until one of the family members returned, Ginger would keep her company.

The brass doors of the lift fanned shut, and while noticeably shuddering, the cables did their job sufficiently in lifting Basil to the rooftop. The lift opened to a long, narrow room, with walls and ceiling made entirely of glass and filled like a thick jungle with greenery and colourful blooms.

Basil called out, "Mr. Murphy?"

Murphy, who'd been examining the leaves of some exotic specimen, seemed lost in thought and didn't respond to Basil's voice. Dressed in the white shirt and black trousers of his standard uniform, Basil noted that the matching black jacket was hanging from a hook near the entrance. Aware of the higher temperatures, Basil pulled at his tie and was tempted but refrained from removing his own jacket.

Murphy was taking care of various plants, gently removing dry bits and watering with a light touch. Basil had never had the patience or desire to keep anything nonhuman alive before and admired those who took such precise care over something that, though beautiful, couldn't return their affection or gratitude. He did recognise a section of elegant orchids and baskets of traditional ferns hanging overhead, but there were many colourful blossoms that he'd never seen before.

"Mr. Murphy," Basil said again.

The butler stopped what he was doing and gave Basil his full attention. Murphy bowed slightly. "Chief Inspector Reed. How can I be of service?"

"You are aware of Mrs. Peck's demise."

"I am, sir. Such a tragedy and on the heels of one so recent."

"The pathologist believes it's poison again."

"That's dreadful, sir."

"Tell me, Murphy, are any of Mr. Peck's plants poisonous?"

Murphy's narrow, dark eyes took in the row of greenery before him. "Well, sir, a goodly amount of that which is beautiful is also toxic if used in a manner it wasn't intended for."

"I'd appreciate it if you spoke clearly on the matter, Mr. Murphy. Which particular species in this conservatory would be lethal if ingested?"

Murphy cast a glance about the room and moved towards a long-stemmed plant with purple hooded flowers. "The wolfsbane, sir. Quite common in these parts."

"What about plants not native to England?"

"Well, there's the oleander, comes from East Asia originally." Murphy pointed to a vibrant plant with pink blossoms that looked as if they'd been flattened in a book. "All parts of this beauty are extremely poisonous. Petals, leaves, stems. If I were you, I wouldn't chance sniffing it."

Basil heeded the butler's caution and stepped back.

"This crawling floral here," Murphy said, enthusiastically, "is clematis. Not as lethal, but still I wouldn't recommend ingesting it."

"Did Mrs. Peck receive a parcel in the post recently?"

Murphy wasn't fazed at the abrupt change of subject. "Yes, sir."

"Can you describe it please?"

"It was rectangular, like a small loaf of bread, if one were packed in a box, sir."

The butler's description matched the scrap of parcel paper Ginger had spotted in the rubbish bin in Mrs. Peck's room.

"Did Mrs. Peck know who the sender was?"

"I don't believe there was a return address, sir."

"Did she guess?"

"Not to my knowledge."

"Did Mrs. Peck know what the parcel was?"

"I heard her take a guess at a tin of tea. She always had her favourite blend sent directly to her. She didn't want anyone else to get into it, I suspect."

"I see. Did you and Mrs. Peck get on, Mr. Murphy?"

"Indeed. She was a fine mistress. Such a shame."

Murphy's manner perplexed Basil. He seemed genuinely shaken by Mrs. Peck's death, yet he appeared to have the greatest access to the conservatory, if indeed the source of the poison was in this room. However, Basil couldn't determine a motive. Like Mrs. McCullagh, if the children didn't keep him on, Murphy had his position to lose.

Any member of the household could've accessed the conservatory and plucked several poisonous leaves. It would have taken several days to dry them to camouflage the dried bits amongst regular tea leaves.

And, how would one get the poison into the parcel of speciality tea?

"Did you see anyone up here whose presence may have surprised you?" Basil asked. "A rare visitor, perhaps?"

"Mrs. Northcott made an appearance last week. Mr. Peck was still alive and rather stunned to find his daughter here. No one, besides myself and Mr. Peck, cared about the rooftop conservatory."

CHAPTER THIRTY-ONE

*A*lthough a discussion over breakfast brought them no closer to a prime suspect, there were other points of interest in the morning papers.

"That Charlie Chaplin film, *The Gold Rush*, releases in the cinemas tomorrow," Ginger said. "I wouldn't mind going to view it sometime."

"There's a rags-to-riches story for you," Basil said. "Mr. Chaplin spent many years in the Lambeth Workhouse as a youngster. His own mother died in a mental institution."

"I definitely want to see his film now. Look at this picture." Ginger held up the newspaper. "He's rather handsome, isn't he?"

"Hmm. I suppose so, though I don't take note of such things."

Ginger's lips twitched as she held in a smile. If

there was one thing she knew about her detective husband, it was that he took note of everything.

Basil put down his teacup. "Look here, Canada House is opening at the end of the month."

"In London?"

"Yes, near Trafalgar Square. I'll drive past it often on my way to work now." Basil glanced up. "I've never been to Canada, have you?"

"I have, once. I went on a business trip with my father when I was thirteen. Toronto and Montreal. I had a bit of a tantrum, simply refusing to be left behind once again with my deplorable stepmother and stepsister." Ginger laughed. "I'm sure I was the deplorable one!"

They pushed their chairs back and moved to the living room. It was time to set their minds back on the case. "Let me bring out my easel and paper," Ginger said. "Haley and I used it often when trying to clear up facts and figures."

Pippins retrieved the items from the store cupboard and set them up in the sitting room. Ginger held a pencil in the air, and Basil sat, one leg crossed over the other, with a coffee cup in hand.

"Means, motive, opportunity," Ginger recited as she wrote the words along the top of the page. "We'll map the information out for Mrs. Peck and cross-reference it with what we know about Mr. Peck."

Basil was grinning when she looked back.

"What is it, darling?"

"Nothing, only I find you adorable when you play the role of governess."

"Happy to entertain you, love."

She wrote down the first name: Cyril Wilding.

"He wanted access to his mother's inheritance," Basil said. "Unless Mrs. Peck had altered her will, he wouldn't have anything to gain by seeing her dead."

"He was incarcerated when her death occurred," Ginger said, "but he could've concocted the poisonous tea and posted it to her earlier, though, according to Mr. Peck's will, her portion upon her death goes to his daughter."

"Which is motive for Deirdre Northcott," Basil said.

Ginger agreed and wrote her name down next.

"All the suspects were capable of poisoning the tea and posting it in advance," Basil said with a disgruntled tone, "which makes nailing down opportunity a blasted difficulty."

"If we agree that all of our suspects had means and opportunity," Ginger said, "it brings us back to motive."

Basil agreed. "At the moment, I'd say Deirdre has the strongest one."

"Matthew Peck didn't want to share his lot with his stepmother," Ginger said. "Perhaps he prefers keeping the business in the family by having his stepmother's shares going to his sister." She jotted down this possible motive.

"Alastair may not have had an official financial gain, but any gain of his wife's was a gain for him."

Ginger wrote the thought down beside Alastair Northcott's name. Not the best marriage, she thought, but unless Deirdre caught her husband in the act of infidelity, and could blame him for a bruise or two, she was rather stuck with him as far as the law went.

She pivoted towards Basil. "Have we ruled out Mrs. McCullagh and Murphy?"

"If we're stating our case on motive, then they are at the bottom of the list."

"On the bottom, yet remaining on the list," Ginger said.

Basil rose to his feet. "We must interview Matthew Peck and the Northcotts again."

CHAPTER THIRTY-TWO

When Ginger and Basil returned to Eaton Square, the Peck residence was in uproar, with one member of the family openly accusing another.

Murphy opened the front door cautiously, and upon seeing a member of the police, invited them inside. Loud, angry voices reverberated through the high ceilings of the entrance, though the creators of this apparently confrontational scene weren't visible. The butler's face was deeply etched with displeasure, though Ginger could tell by the twitching around his mouth he meant to keep his professional demeanour, despite the chaotic environment.

"Mr. Peck and Mr. and Mrs. Northcott are in the drawing room," Murphy said. "Shall I announce your arrival?"

"No need," Basil said. Ginger concurred with Basil's nonconventional presentation. She wanted to overhear the argument as well.

Deirdre Northcott's voice rose above the others. "I'm now the majority shareholder of Papa's business holdings, so you shall answer to me!"

"Had Father known Virginia was going to kick the bucket so soon—" This from Matthew Peck— "he'd not have made such a concession. I'm speaking to my solicitor to have the will contested."

"Contested?" Alastair Northcott's contempt was loud and clear.

Matthew Peck's voice returned, "It's obvious that Father wasn't of sound mind."

"How dare you?" Deirdre Northcott replied. "If Papa had wanted you to have control of his company, he'd have clearly named you. We both know he didn't trust your business instincts.

"And you think he trusts yours?" Matthew Peck said.

"I'm not about to waste it on risky investments."

"I think you underestimate your sister, Matthew," Alastair Northcott chimed in. "Besides, whilst on the topic of sound minds—"

"You!" Matthew Peck was shouting now. "You can bloody well stay out of it! You don't know a thing about the state of my mind. How grand for you to have missed out on the battle, protected by some fancy desk job, you gigantic milksop! Don't think I'll stand by whilst you try to run my business through my sister's name!"

"You're mad!" Alastair Northcott yelled.

Matthew Peck responded, "Don't you dare call me 'mad', old man!"

This outburst was followed by the sound of glass breaking.

Ginger and Basil shared a look. They'd better interrupt before there was a third murder to investigate.

Basil pushed open the door and shocked the occupants into silence.

"Gentlemen, Mrs. Northcott," Basil said genially. "So sorry to interrupt your family meeting. Do you mind telling me what's going on?"

Deirdre stood with the pieces of a broken vase in either hand. "Nothing at all. I clumsily knocked this onto the floor."

"I see," Basil said. He tugged on his waistcoat. "As you well know, we've got two murder enquiries on the go now. I'll need to interview each of you once again, separately. Mrs. Northcott, let's start with you."

CHAPTER THIRTY-THREE

*D*eidre sniffed. "I want to speak to Mrs. Reed alone."

"I'm afraid you'll have to make do with both of us," Basil replied.

"I don't even know why you've come," she said. "You have your killer already."

"Mr. Wilding was being held overnight," Ginger responded. "He couldn't have killed Mrs. Peck."

"He had no idea when Virginia was going to drink that tea. He could've spiked it anytime."

"What makes you think she was poisoned?" Basil asked.

Mrs. Northcott stammered, "It was just speculation. I assumed . . . since my father's death. . ." Her voice trailed off.

"Even so," Basil said, "Why would you think the poison was in the tea?"

Deirdre glanced at him with a startled expression. "How else could it have been administered?"

"Well, since we don't know the nature of the poison, should that be the cause of death, we can't really say definitively," Ginger said. "She may have been poked with something, or perhaps the poison was absorbed through her skin."

Deirdre appeared sincerely rattled. "That hadn't occurred to me. Just the timing—oh, Lord, you don't think my husband did it?"

"Rather," Basil said with an inclination of his head, "we think it might've been you."

Deirdre swallowed hard, and her large eyes glistened. "It wasn't me, I swear. I know Virginia said that awful thing about having to watch her back, and I do realise I have the greatest motive. Oh, dear, why would Papa do that to me? He must've known what it would look like to place me in that position."

"Perhaps he didn't think one of his children would murder his wife," Basil said, "at least not so soon after his death."

"This whole situation is beastly!"

"If you didn't kill your stepmother," Basil said, "who do you think did?"

"I don't know. What an impossible position. It must've been Murphy. Yes!" She glared back as if accusing the faithful servant was the answer to all her problems. "It's usually the butler in these sorts of situations, isn't it?"

"What motive would Mr. Murphy have for killing your father and his wife?" Ginger asked. "He wasn't even mentioned in the will."

"Oh, yes, well." Mrs. Northcott stared down at the crumpled handkerchief in her hand. "I suppose that was rather mean of Papa, wasn't it? Especially for Murphy. Papa could've thrown a few quid his way."

"Do you think Matthew capable of such a crime?"

Mrs. Northcott stiffened. "No. Matthew has a temper, the war did that to him, you see, but he loved Papa, no matter their differences. And Papa was dying anyway."

"What about Mrs. Peck?"

Mrs. Northcott shook her head sharply. "No. Matthew's not a killer. He even hated shooting the Germans. He was reprimanded for his lack of commitment in that regard, and had the war not ended when it did, he might've been court-martialled."

She took a deep breath then stared hard at Ginger and Basil. "It was Alastair. He killed them."

Ginger gasped at Deirdre's proclamation. It would've been quite acceptable for Mrs. Northcott to simply say she didn't know, but when the choice was so bluntly put before her, her brother or her husband, Deirdre's loyalty was clear.

"That's a serious accusation to make against your husband," Ginger said. "Do you have any proof?"

"Not directly. He left the bedroom the night Papa was killed. We haven't shared a bed since then."

They were interrupted by Constable Braxton. "Excuse me, sir, but a call came in from the Yard, and they've received a report from the mortuary."

Basil walked across the room and claimed the folded piece of paper. Ginger joined him, and Basil handed the note to her.

"Oleander?" she said quietly.

Basil confirmed softly in return. "Yes. Both Reginald and Virginia Peck were poisoned with the plant."

"Which could be dried and mixed with tea leaves," Ginger whispered. She perused the note again. "In Reginald's case, Dr. Gupta now believes the poison was administered slowly over time, and the cumulative effect finally killed him. Whereas, Virginia had a stronger dose."

"Mr. Peck and Murphy grow oleander in the conservatory," Basil said. "I'm told it's very poisonous, including the leaves. Someone went to the trouble of putting minute amounts of the poison into Reginald's daily tea."

"But showed no restraint with Virginia," Ginger

added. "And how did they get it into the parcel Mrs. Peck received in the post?"

Basil excused Constable Braxton. "Make sure to keep Mr. Peck and Mr. Northcott in the house."

Ginger and Basil stepped back to where they'd left Deirdre Northcott.

"Mrs. Northcott," Basil said. "We have a witness that you were seen in the conservatory last week."

"Murphy, of course. Why?"

"Just answer the question, Mrs. Northcott."

"I visited my father. It's not so unusual."

"Except you rarely went up to the conservatory, isn't that correct?"

"Murphy told you that? Well, I knew Papa was dying. I had to go to where he was if I wanted to see him, and if he wasn't in his room, he was almost always in the conservatory." She added defensively, "Just because Murphy didn't see anyone besides me, doesn't mean anything. Murphy's not up there all the time, and besides, wouldn't the murderer take special care not to be seen?"

GINGER AND BASIL left Mrs. Northcott in the care of Sergeant Scott, and at Basil's request, Alastair North-cott was ushered into the sitting room.

"It's hard to tell if Mrs. Northcott believes her

brother is guilty," Ginger said quietly, "and is trying to protect him, or if she sincerely believes her husband to be guilty."

"If she was covering for Matthew Peck," Basil said, "why she's worked so hard to cast suspicion on everyone else would make sense."

Alastair Northcott seemed to understand the seriousness of the situation and had left his Indian *kurta* behind in favour of a classic English suit.

Ginger watched as Basil got straight to the point.

"Mr. Northcott, your wife believes you capable of murder."

Alastair Northcott's expression crumpled as he let out a gasp. "I'm not falling for your tricks, Chief Inspector."

"What do you mean by that?" Basil asked.

"You want me to say something in my defence that would implicate me. My wife isn't stable in her mind. In fact, I've yet to meet a Peck who is. If you're looking for a killer, I'd say Matthew is your man."

Ginger found the mudslinging tiresome. He said, she said. What they needed was a real clue!

"When was the last time you were in the conservatory, Mr. Northcott?" she asked.

"So long ago, I couldn't even say. Perhaps before Deirdre and I left for India."

"You'd testify to that under oath?" Basil said.

"Indeed. I'm not a plant man. Quite honestly, I can't get my tongue around the names. Mr. Peck found a lot of solace in them, I'm told, not that it was much help to him."

"Are you a tea drinker?" Ginger asked.

Mr. Northcott shot her a strange look. "I'm British. Of course, I'm a tea drinker."

"I meant, rather, do you like exotic teas?"

"That was one thing I couldn't adapt to, I'm afraid, while abroad," Mr. Northcott said. "Give me a good black tea as opposed to some sweetened Indian chai any day." He narrowed his eyes in thought. "It's true, then is it? Virginia's tea was poisoned? I'm assuming, in light of the nature of your questions."

"In fact, it's Reginald Peck's death that has been confirmed," Basil said. "Did you and Mrs. Peck get on?"

"Probably more so than anyone else in this infernal house. Apart from Mr. Wilding, when he joined us. Is the bounder still under arrest?"

"For the time being," Basil said. "We've yet to determine if we're after one killer or two."

Alastair Northcott let out a dry chuckle. "What are the odds? Between you, me, and the fence post, I wish I'd never married into this loony family. If you're wondering why I ran off to India, this is why. Loony, I say."

Ginger sympathised with Mr. Northcott. Ambrosia could be difficult and at times unreasonable, but she remained endearing, and never spiteful, unlike her new in-laws appeared to be. If the Northcotts and the servants were innocent, then it really did look as if Matthew Peck was the guilty party. What they needed was a confession.

Ginger spoke softly in Basil's direction. "Shall we interview Mr. Peck now?"

Basil nodded just as the door burst open and startled the three of them. Matthew Peck stepped inside, his hair messy and his collar open. His eyes blazed with the anger of a man in emotional turmoil. In his hand was a long-nosed revolver, the kind Ginger had seen often in France. He raised it slowly and pointed it at Alastair Northcott.

CHAPTER THIRTY-FOUR

*B*asil slowly raised a palm. "Steady on, old bean."

Matthew's hand shook as he waved the army weapon between them. "Don't move!"

Alastair Northcott seemed to have enough sense to be frightened. "What on earth are you doing, Matthew? You're mad. Don't be a lunatic."

Mr. Peck spoke in eerie staccato. "Don't call me mad."

"What is going on in here?" Deirdre Northcott strolled into the room, not realising at first the seriousness of the situation. When her focus latched on to the weapon, her eyes widened. "Matthew?"

"Stay back, Deirdre, or I'll shoot."

"Matthew?" Deirdre repeated. "Don't be ridiculous. Who exactly are you going to shoot?"

Matthew Peck realigned his aim towards Mr. Northcott.

"Alastair?" Deirdre scoffed. "What on earth for?"

"He doesn't belong here," Matthew Peck said, his voice thin with emotion. "He doesn't belong in our family. Walking around in foreign pyjamas, chanting, and meditating—he brings disgrace to the Peck name."

"That's not worth killing him over," Deirdre said.

Ginger worried that Mr. Peck, with his shaky hand, might pull the trigger without intent. "Perhaps, Mr. Peck, you could put the pistol down, and we can discuss matters civilly."

"Civilly? This man is a murderer! He killed Father and now Virginia. Who's next? Me? Deirdre?"

"I don't know who killed Reginald and Virginia," Alastair Northcott said, his hands high in defence, "but it wasn't me."

"Shut up!"

"Stop it, Matthew!" Mrs. Northcott demanded. "If you shoot my husband, I'll never forgive you!"

Deirdre appeared to have some influence on her brother because his hand now wavered.

Ginger permitted a breath of relief to escape, but it proved to be premature.

Deirdre stepped forward.

Matthew pointed the gun at his own head.

Deirdre screamed, "Matthew!"

The door opened, which drew the attention of the room.

Alastair Northcott jumped to his feet.

The gun went off.

CHAPTER THIRTY-FIVE

Ohen Constable Braxton had entered the sitting room to deliver a message, he had no idea about the drama that had been unfolding. Ginger had almost swallowed her heart when Matthew Peck turned the gun on himself. The split-second distraction the constable had created was long enough for Alastair Northcott to jump on Mr. Peck to save his life.

Basil was quick to detain Matthew Peck. "Braxton, get the cuffs."

The attention of the room shifted to Mr. Peck's arrest. It was a moment before Deirdre's moan caught Ginger's attention. Mrs. Northcott held a hand to her left arm. Blood oozed through her fingertips.

"We need a doctor!" Ginger said. "Mrs. Northcott's been hit."

"I'll see to it," Constable Braxton said.

Ginger commandeered Basil's tie. "We need to stop the blood flow."

Deirdre Northcott winced as Ginger wrapped the tie above the wound and pulled.

"Deirdre!" Alastair Northcott looked as if he'd barely processed his own close call when he realised his wife had been injured.

"It's just a flesh wound," she said with a whimper.

"Maybe so, but you're going to need stitches." Ginger never verbalised her thought that Mrs. Northcott was fortunate the shot hadn't been a couple of inches to the left. A bullet to the heart would've killed her on the spot.

There was so much commotion. Basil contained the area and preserved the scene. The doctor arrived. Mrs. Northcott was carried out. Then, with the arrest and detainment of Mr. Peck, the person who was the object of the message, was temporarily overlooked.

"Mr. Winthrop," Basil said. The solicitor, who had been seated on a chair in the foyer, briefcase covering his lap, got to his feet.

"Chief Inspector, I see I've arrived at a most inopportune time. I hope Mrs. Northcott's injuries aren't serious?"

"The doctor says she will recover," Basil said.

"Mr. Northcott rang with the news about Mrs. Peck's unfortunate demise."

Basil rubbed the back of his neck. "Yes, well, we're rather busy at the moment."

"I do hate to interrupt," Mr. Winthrop said, "and I wouldn't have bothered if I didn't think it of immense importance."

Ginger had approached near the end of Mr. Winthrop's plea. "Please, do come with us," she said.

Once they were seated in the sitting room, Basil asked, "What is it that you have to report?"

"Whilst Mr. Peck was alive, he believed that someone was trying to kill him."

"Yes," Basil said, "you stated that the other day. What does this have to do with the death of Virginia Peck?"

"Well, one of Mr. Peck's instructions for me, a task he insisted I do immediately after his death, was to send a parcel to his wife."

Ginger arched a brow. "That was what you were doing when we accompanied you to the post office?"

"Yes."

"Was the item a tin of tea?" Ginger asked. She held out her hands to form a rectangle. "About this size?"

"It was. It was Mrs. Peck's favourite, and Mr. Peck wanted the gift sent to her as a comforting gesture. At least, that is what he told me."

"But . . ." Ginger prompted. She had a sinking feeling Mr. Peck's intentions were less gracious."

"Mr. Peck believed someone was poisoning him," Mr. Winthrop repeated. "I now believe he suspected his wife."

Basil glanced at Ginger before asking, "Are you saying that you believe that Virginia Peck poisoned Mr. Peck, and Mr. Peck, in turn, poisoned his wife?" Ginger asked.

The solicitor shrugged, and Ginger gasped. What a shocking revelation!

"Why?" Basil asked. "What motive did she have to want to kill her husband when he was already dying."

"I can offer a guess," Mr. Winthrop said. "Reginald all but ignored his wife, saving his attention and charms for his business employees and associates. I tried to tell him he was asking for trouble."

"Is that what you were arguing about at the gala?" Ginger asked.

Mr. Winthrop settled his gaze on her. "You saw that, did you? Yes. I could see Mrs. Peck stewing. Her eyes were filled with disdain when she stared at her husband. If she wanted to get out of the marriage, well. . ."

"If I might ask," began Basil, "what business was it of yours if a client got on with his wife or not?"

"I worried about a potential scandal. Reginald had

a sterling reputation. I didn't want to see it tarnished at the end of his life. Looks like I was helpless to stop it."

"If what you say is true," Ginger said, "then Reginald was the revengeful sort. How did he do it with no one knowing?"

"I can only assume that he dried the leaves and petals of his toxic plant of choice and added them to the tin before giving it to me as a provision," Mr. Winthrop said.

Basil let out a long breath then asked, "Why are you coming to us with this now?"

"Because of the suddenness of Mrs. Peck's death. Am I right? Was she poisoned by an exotic floral?"

"I hate to play the devil's advocate," Basil said, "but how can we be sure that you didn't poison Mrs. Peck's tea?"

Mr. Winthrop's jaw dropped. "Why would I do that?"

"Revenge, perhaps?" Ginger offered. It was a stretch, but stranger things had proven true. "You strongly believe she killed your client?"

"If that were the case, I wouldn't be sitting here right now telling you how it was done. Besides, I have this."

Mr. Winthrop pulled out a folded piece of paper from his briefcase. "It's a signed and stamped addendum from Mr. Peck indicating his wishes. His instructions about the tea are clear. I wish now I'd followed my instinct and just thrown the blasted thing out."

The solicitor handed Basil the document, and once Basil had read it, he gave the paper to Ginger.

"It certainly seems that Mr. Peck had thought ahead," Ginger said. "What a bizarre twist."

CHAPTER THIRTY-SIX

"It's like a reverse Romeo and Juliet." Felicia waved her arms with flair. "Instead of sharing poison out of love, they shared it from hate."

Ginger and Basil were partaking of an after-dinner drink with Felicia and Ambrosia. Boss claimed his spot on Ginger's lap and she rhythmically stroked her pet's fur.

"Both situations are tragic."

"I, for one, don't think true love is an excuse for ending a life," Ambrosia said. "If you love someone, you're hardly going to let them drink poison."

"It's called a romantic tragedy, Grandmama." Felicia rolled her large eyes. "And I hardly think we're in a position to question Shakespeare."

"And why not?" Ambrosia postured. "He's only famous because he's been dead for three centuries.

One can hardly make sense of his plays, and I don't know why civilised people harp on about him so."

"Though not romantic, this case is certainly tragic," Ginger said. "Mr. Peck's final violent act against his wife almost resulted in the death of his son by suicide, and then of his daughter by accidental shooting."

"Poor Matthew Peck," Felicia whimpered. "What's going to happen to him now?"

Basil, looking as if he'd resigned himself to silence as the Gold ladies dominated the conversation, cleared his throat. "Mr. Peck is to be remanded for brandishing a loaded and unregistered weapon. The pistol, having been issued by the crown for the war effort, will be returned to the crown."

Ginger knew that many crown-issued weapons had been reported missing in France only to mysteriously appear in Britain.

Basil continued, "Mr. Peck is currently under the care of the police surgeon and is being given psychiatric care."

"At least Mrs. Northcott is recovering," Ginger said. "She has her father's business to run now."

"Mr. Peck must've suspected that his son had returned from the war in a damaged state," Felicia said, "to have given his daughter controlling shares."

Ginger agreed. To favour a daughter over a son was quite unorthodox.

"I still can't get over the fact that the wife killed her husband and the husband, after his death, killed his wife," Felicia said. "I couldn't make that up, and I write mysteries!"

"To paraphrase Lord Byron," Ginger added, "truth is stranger than fiction."

"At least Mr. Wilding has been exonerated," Felicia said sympathetically. "What a traumatic time he's had. Firstly, finding his natural mother, just to lose her in such a dreadful manner."

"It turns out that Virginia Peck had a will," Basil said, "and though she wasn't in possession of a fortune, she left everything in her name to Mr. Wilding. It'll give him a step up, if he's wise with it."

"She loved her son, and would do anything to protect him," Ginger replied with newfound understanding. "She could've got away with murder, instead she confessed to the crime even though it surely meant she'd go to the gallows."

"I admit, I thought Mrs. Northcott was in on it," Basil said. "She seemed quite determined to cast suspicion on everyone else."

"Except her brother," Ginger said. "I'm quite convinced she believed him to be guilty."

Basil agreed. "I imagine she hoped to keep the waters muddy, so that we couldn't, in the end, arrest anyone."

. . .

LATER, when they said goodnight and dispersed to make ready for bed, Ginger slipped into Scout's room. She hovered quietly over the boy's bed and watched him breathe. She sensed that the time they had left together before he morphed from his angelic childlike state into an awkward young man, was short. Somehow, it mattered not to Ginger, and her desire to care for, protect, and guide this soul into a hopeful future only grew more significant with each day.

How awful of Mr. and Mrs. Reed to force her to choose between a child and her husband?

With all that had been going on with the Peck case, they'd hardly had time to discuss the situation— perhaps the truth was, neither wanted to broach the uncomfortable subject. Basil didn't share the parental feelings Ginger had for Scout; she knew this. Not that he had an ill attitude towards him, just not deep feelings. He accepted Scout's presence and the part he played in Ginger's life because he loved Ginger.

Could she expect him to give up his inheritance for a child he didn't genuinely love?

What a beastly situation she found herself in.

She let out a sorrowful sigh before tiptoeing out of Scout's room.

"What's the matter, my love," Basil said when Ginger joined him in their bed. She'd changed into a jade silk negligee, but couldn't shake the melancholy she carried.

"I feel I'm in the horrible situation of having to choose between two loves. My husband or my son."

Basil pulled Ginger close and placed a hand on her chin, forcing her to look him in the eye. "Since we both came into your life at the same time, I can hardly claim seniority."

Ginger felt a chill shoot through her. "What are you saying?" He wasn't about to tell her he was leaving, was he?

"I'm saying that it would be wrong for me to make you choose, and though I can't help what my parents decide, my choice was never in question."

"What's your choice?" Ginger whispered.

"My choice is you, of course. You and Scout."

The relief Ginger felt was immense, and she needed a moment to catch her breath.

"But what about your inheritance?" she finally asked. She couldn't believe Basil would walk away from a considerable amount of money without a seed of doubt.

"Have you forgotten our vows already, Mrs. Reed? For richer or for poorer?"

He sealed his words with a tender kiss, and Ginger

couldn't have loved him more than she did in that instant. Her, Basil, and Scout.

She whispered softly. "The three of us are a family."

Boss jumped on the bed at that moment, and looked at her with his dark perceptive eyes.

Ginger smiled. "I meant the four of us, Bossy."

The End

If you enjoyed reading *Murder on Eaton Square* please help others enjoy it too.

Recommend it: Help others find the book by recommending it to friends, readers' groups, discussion boards and by **suggesting it to your local library.**

Review it: Please tell other readers why you liked this book by reviewing it on Amazon or Goodreads.

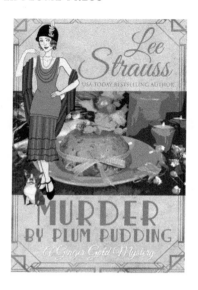

MURDER BY PLUM PUDDING

There's nothing more fun than a festive holiday dinner party and Ginger Reed, the former Lady Gold, has Hartigan House decorated and the gramophone playing. Dressed in her finest Parisian low-waisted gown, feather-topped tiara, and T-strapped Italian leather shoes, Ginger is ready to host the delectable event.

It's a jolly good time, until someone chokes on the *pudding*.

Is it an accident or is it murder? And can Ginger unravel the mystery before the church bells ring and Christmas Day dawns?

Introducing LADY GOLD INVESTIGATES!

Ginger Gold has opened her own private investigation office!

This short story companion series to Ginger Gold Mysteries has the clever Mrs. Ginger Reed, aka Lady Gold, and her adventurous sister-in-law Felicia taking on clients who've got all sorts of troubles. This first volume consists of *The Case of the Wayward Wife*, and *The Case of the Boy who Vanished*.

A companion series to Ginger Gold

Mysteries, each volume is approximately 20 thousand words or 90 pages. A bite size read perfect for a transit commute home, time spent waiting at an appointment, or to settle into sleep at night. Get your coffee, tea or glass of wine and snuggle in!

ON AMAZON
or order from your favorite bookstore.

Check out Volume 2 with *The Case of the Missing Recipe* and *The Case of the Museum Heist*

READ ON FOR AN EXCERPT OF *The Case of the Vanishing Boy*

Book #12 in Ginger Gold Mysteries coming soon!

Murder's a Deadly Secret

Mrs. Ginger Reed—the former Lady Gold—thought her past was dead and buried, but when the mysterious death of a British Secret Service agent threatens to expose her own Great War secrets, she's faced with an unimaginable dilemma: break her legal vow to the Official Secrets Act or join the agency again, something she's loathed to do.

Because once they own your soul, there's no getting it back.

Visit leestraussbooks.com for updates and more information!

GINGER GOLD'S JOURNAL

Sign up for Lee's readers list and gain access to **Ginger Gold's private Journal.** Find out about Ginger's Life before the SS *Rosa* and how she became the woman she has. This is a fluid document that will cover her romance with her late husband Daniel, her time serving in the British secret service during World War One, and beyond. Includes a recipe for Dark Dutch Chocolate Cake!

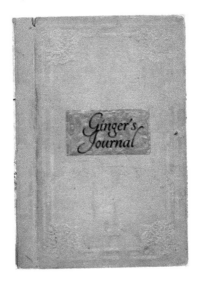

It begins: **July 31, 1912**

How fabulous that I found this Journal today, hidden in the bottom of my wardrobe. Good old Pippins, our English butler in London, gave it to me as a parting gift when Father whisked me away on our American adventure so he could marry Sally. Pips said it was for me to record my new adventures. I'm ashamed I never even penned one word before today. I think I was just too sad.

This old leather-bound journal takes me back to that emotional time. I had shed enough tears to fill the ocean and I remember telling Father dramatically that I was certain to cause flooding to match God's. At eight years old I was well-trained in my biblical studies, though, in retro-spect, I would say that I had probably bordered on heresy with my little tantrum.

The first week of my "adventure" was spent with a tummy ache and a number of embarrassing sessions that involved a bucket and Father holding back my long hair so I wouldn't soil it with vomit.

I certainly felt that I was being punished for some reason. Hartigan House—though large and sometimes lonely—was my home and Pips was my good friend. He often helped me to pass the time with games of I Spy and Xs and Os.

"Very good, Little Miss," he'd say with a twinkle in his blue eyes when I won, which I did often. I suspect now that our good butler wasn't beyond letting me win even when unmerited.

Father had got it into his silly head that I needed a mother, but I think the truth was he wanted a wife. Sally, a woman half my father's age, turned out to be a sufficient wife in the end, but I could never claim her as a mother.

Well, Pips, I'm sure you'd be happy to

know that things turned out all right here in America.

Subscribe to read more!
leestraussbooks.com

.

LADY GOLD INVESTIGATES (Ginger Gold companion short stories)

Volume 1

Volume 2

Volume 3

HIGGINS & HAWKE MYSTERY SERIES (cozy 1930s historical)

The 1930s meets Rizzoli & Isles in this friendship depression era cozy mystery series.

Death at the Tavern

Death on the Tower

Death on Hanover

A NURSERY RHYME MYSTERY SERIES(mystery/sci fi)

Marlow finds himself teamed up with intelligent and savvy Sage Farrell, a girl so far out of his league he feels blinded in her presence - literally - damned glasses! Together they work to find the identity of @gingerbreadman. Can they stop the killer before he strikes again?

Gingerbread Man

Life Is but a Dream

Hickory Dickory Dock

Twinkle Little Star

THE PERCEPTION TRILOGY (YA dystopian mystery)

Zoe Vanderveen is a GAP—a genetically altered person. She lives in the security of a walled city on prime water-front property along side other equally beautiful people with extended life spans. Her brother Liam is missing. Noah Brody, a boy on the outside, is the only one who can help ∼ but can she trust him?

Perception

Volition

Contrition

LIGHT & LOVE (sweet romance)

Set in the dazzling charm of Europe, follow Katja, Gabriella, Eva, Anna and Belle as they find strength, hope and love.

Sing me a Love Song

Your Love is Sweet

In Light of Us

Lying in Starlight

PLAYING WITH MATCHES (WW2

history/romance)

A sobering but hopeful journey about how one young Germany boy copes with the war and propaganda. Based on true events.

A Piece of Blue String (companion short story)

THE CLOCKWISE COLLECTION (YA time travel romance)

Casey Donovan has issues: hair, height and uncontrollable trips to the 19th century! And now this ~ she's accidentally taken Nate Mackenzie, the cutest boy in the school, back in time. Awkward.

Clockwise

Clockwiser

Like Clockwork

Counter Clockwise

Clockwork Crazy

Clocked (companion novella)

Standalones

As Elle Lee Strauss

Seaweed

Love, Tink

ABOUT THE AUTHOR

Lee Strauss is a USA TODAY bestselling author of The Ginger Gold Mysteries series, The Higgins & Hawke Mystery series (cozy historical mysteries), A Nursery Rhyme Mystery series (mystery suspense), The Perception series (young adult dystopian), The Light & Love series (sweet romance), The Clockwise Collection (YA time travel romance), and young adult historical fiction with over a million books read. She has titles published in German, Spanish and Korean, and a growing audio library.

When Lee's not writing or reading she likes to cycle, hike, and play pickleball. She loves to drink caffè lattes and red wines in exotic places, and eat dark chocolate anywhere.

For more info on books by Lee Strauss and her social media links, visit leestraussbooks.com. To make sure you don't miss the next new release, be sure to sign up for her readers' list!

Did you know you can follow your favourite authors on Bookbub? If you subscribe to Bookbub — (and if you don't, why don't you? - They'll send you daily emails alerting you to sales and new releases on just the kind of books you like to read!) — follow me to make sure you don't miss the next Ginger Gold Mystery!

www.leestraussbooks.com
leestraussbooks@gmail.com

THE CASE OF THE VANISHING BOY -
CHAPTER 1

The black and cream cradle telephone that sat on the counter of Ginger's Regent Street dress shop rang just as Ginger stepped inside. Madame Roux, her efficient shop manager, was busy with a customer—a tall, aristocratic-looking lady with a penchant for Schiaparelli.

She removed her gloves and placed them and her handbag behind the counter, then picked up the receiver and sang into it, "Good morning, Feathers and Flair. How may I help you?"

"Ginger?"

"Oliver!" She immediately recognised the voice of her friend Reverend, Oliver Hill.

"Yes. It's so good to hear your voice. I hope you're well."

"I'm doing quite well, thank you." Ginger was

genuinely pleased to hear from the gentle vicar, though she was rather curious as to why he would seek her out at her shop. "I hope things are well with you too. Do tell me how things are at the church?"

One of the joys in Ginger's life was the Child Wellness Project that she had initiated with Oliver. The charity's main focus was feeding nutritious meals to street children twice a week, at the hall of St. George's Church.

"Everything is running as smoothly as can be expected. Numbers are up, and so are donations. We continue to have sufficient volunteers to help serve and cook the meals for the project, and lately there have even been some food donations from bakeries and grocers. I am quite encouraged."

"Oh, that is wonderful!"

"However, I have a concern that perhaps you can help with."

"Of course." Ginger retrieved a pencil and paper from under the counter. Finally, to the mystery behind Oliver's call.

"There is a young boy named Eddie, nine years old. I don't know his last name but he has been coming for meals for a quite a while now."

"The blond lad with the chipped front tooth?" Ginger asked. "Such an adorable youngster. I have had several amusing conversations with him. Boss just simply adores him. In fact they have become good friends." The child reminded her of Scout, her ward who had once lived on the streets. Scout was now a much-loved member of her household at Hartigan House, and though it had initially taken some adjustment for everyone, taking him in was something she had never come to regret. It was always inspiring to her how many of these young street children had such bright personalities and charm despite their sad circumstances in life. It broke Ginger's heart to see their innocence eroded much too early by the harshness of their existence.

"Yes, that's the one," Oliver replied. "Quite a bright young lad and very friendly. Some of the ladies who serve food are rather taken with him and have got to know him a little."

Ginger's heart pinched with worry. "Has something happened to Eddie?"

"It seems that he has gone missing."

"Oh mercy. Can you meet me right away at my office at Lady Gold Investigations? I want to give this my full attention until we find him again."

Oliver's answer was resolute. "I can be there in half an hour."

Get it on Amazon
or order from your favortie bookstore.

ACKNOWLEDGMENTS

Special thanks to Heather Belleguelle for her insights on family history research during turn of the century London, and for being an awesome person to work with, always willing to go the extra mile.

Lightning Source UK Ltd.
Milton Keynes UK
UKHW012250110821
388699UK00004B/1204

9 781774 090398